HER GAME, THE

The Martinis and Chocolate Book Club 2

Lara Valentine

MENAGE EVERLASTING

Siren Publishing, Inc.
www.SirenPublishing.com

A SIREN PUBLISHING BOOK
IMPRINT: Ménage Everlasting

HER GAME, THEIR RULES
Copyright © 2012 by Lara Valentine

ISBN: 978-1-62241-819-0

First Printing: October 2012

Cover design by Les Byerley
All art and logo copyright © 2012 by Siren Publishing, Inc.

Printed in the U.S.A.

PUBLISHER
Siren Publishing, Inc.
www.SirenPublishing.com

DEDICATION

For my sister

HER GAME, THEIR RULES

The Martinis and Chocolate
Book Club 2

LARA VALENTINE
Copyright © 2012

Chapter 1

"I'm not really sure what you need me to do, Mr. Martin. I can't be overdrawn."

Sara Jameson juggled her purse, her car keys, her diaper bag, and her almost-two-year-old son, Jack, before dropping into a guest chair across from the very nervous-looking bank employee. This stop was the first of many today. It was going to be a long day. She needed to get Jack to preschool so she could run the myriad of errands she had saved. The call from the bank had been unexpected, and now she was trying to squeeze this errand in with all the others.

"No, no, Mrs. Jameson. It's just that, well, this is an unusual matter. I wanted to speak to you in person."

Mr. Martin looked very uncomfortable. She knew that as a widow, especially a young widow, she often made people uncomfortable. They never seemed to know what to say after they found out her marital state. She had been married for five years to a wonderful man.

Scott had been taken unexpectedly fourteen months ago by a rare, undiagnosed heart defect. They had never known they were living on borrowed time. They had so many dreams that would go unfulfilled.

However, one dream they had achieved was tugging at her hair and dropping cereal bar crumbs on her once-pristine white blouse—Jack.

"What *is* the unusual matter, then?"

"Well, one of your husband's accounts has a zero balance. We need to know whether you want us to transfer funds into that account and continue the monthly fund transfers."

Sara frowned. "Zero balance? Fund transfers? I don't understand, Mr. Martin. My husband and I had a joint checking account and joint savings account, which reverted to me upon his death. If I'm not overdrawn, then how can our balance be zero?"

Mr. Martin fidgeted in his chair. "Your husband had an account in his name only. I looked into the history of the account in preparation for this meeting. The account has been open for four years. Your husband deposited twenty-five thousand dollars in the account every January. The reason no red flag was raised before this is that the account had funds in it for the transfer."

Twenty-five thousand dollars? That was a lot of money. Scott had been paid extremely well. He was a partner in his family's very successful business. Still, why would he deposit that kind of money in an account?

"How could Scott have an account that I didn't know about? We never received a statement." Sara was sure this was a mistake.

"Your husband had the statements sent to an e-mail address. This one." Mr. Martin handed over a small piece of paper. Sara shook her head.

"I don't recognize this e-mail address. You say the account is at zero? Where has the money gone? I didn't spend it."

When Scott had died the finances had been in pristine condition. No unpaid bills were found, the mortgage was up-to-date, and the savings account was healthy. Scott had been extremely conscientious about taking care of his family.

"Each month, a two-thousand-dollar fund transfer was made to a bank account in Champaign, Illinois. Do you know anyone in Champaign, Illinois, Mrs. Jameson?"

Sara sighed in relief. "Yes, I do. My husband is originally from Champaign, and his brother still lives there and runs the family business. Scott worked remotely for the company. This account probably has something to do with the business."

She and Scott weren't short any funds so the money must belong to the company. Sara shifted Jack to her other knee. He was behaving beautifully, but as soon as the cereal bar was gone, he would be squirming and raring to go.

Mr. Martin looked relieved. "Ah, excellent. Do you want me to transfer funds to that account then? We can get the paperwork together to transfer the account to you if you like."

Sara was anxious to get going. "Yes, go ahead and transfer the funds for this month. I'll call my brother-in-law today and find out what the account is for. I'm sure Jeremy will be able to take care of this before we need to worry about next month's transfer."

Jeremy, Scott's older brother, could take care of just about anything. He was one of the most competent men she had ever met. It was too bad he didn't want to run for president. He had made the family business one of the most successful video game companies in the country. Jeremy was the brains behind the business. Jeremy's partner and husband, Cole, was the artistic genius, and Scott had been the sales talent. The three of them had built a very successful video game company.

Jeremy was also one of the kindest men she had ever met. He and Cole had stayed with her for an entire month after Scott's death. Even now, they talked on Skype every Sunday.

Mr. Martin was smiling now. "After you talk to your brother-in-law, please just call me and let me know how you want to handle this going forward. I do appreciate your coming in to talk to me today."

"Talk!" Crumbs went flying out of Jack's mouth.

Sara smiled at her son and pulled a wet wipe out of her purse to clean up his face.

"Yes, Jack. Mommy came to talk to Mr. Martin. We're going bye-bye, now. Say bye-bye."

"Bye-bye." Jack smiled, showing pearly white front teeth.

"He looks just like you."

Sara shook her head. "Except for his hair, he looks like Scott, actually. I don't see the resemblance."

"He does resemble you. Very much."

Sara knew that Mr. Martin was trying to be kind.

"Well, thank you. He's a handsome boy."

Jack was handsome. He had her dark hair and Scott's striking blue eyes.

"C'mon, Jack. I'm taking you to preschool."

"Pee-skool." Jack grinned.

Sara grabbed up her belongings and headed to the parking lot. She needed to get all those errands done, and now a call to Jeremy had been added to the list.

* * * *

Their hands were everywhere at once. Luke's rough fingertips stroked her hard nipples while Tom's digits fucked her sopping pussy. Each stroke was like a wire tugging at her clit, making her shake and moan with arousal. Luke leaned down to capture her lips with his own. His mouth dominated hers, his tongue sweeping her mouth as if he owned it. In a way, he did. She couldn't have stopped him if she tried. They both played her body like fine musicians.

She reached down and cupped the bulge in his jeans. His cock hardened further under her palm. She rubbed the outline of his erection until he groaned against her mouth.

"It's all for you, baby. I can't wait to bury my cock in your cunt. You're going to be screaming my name before this night is over."

"Pretty sure of himself, isn't he?" Noelle teased.

"Does she even know his name? She just met him! I don't care how good he smells." Sara popped another Godiva in her mouth. She'd missed lunch running errands.

"I feel bad for Tom. He's doing the hard work but not getting any attention." Lisa smirked.

"There's always the unsung hero." Brianne smiled.

"I wouldn't mind two or three men doing me." Tori laughed. Her eyes had lost their shadowed look. It was now more than two years since her own husband had died after a long battle with cancer.

The women shrieked in laughter at Tori's outrageous statement. Their book club met once a week to read some fun smut, eat fine chocolate, and have a girly cocktail. Needless to say, the women had become close friends and had few secrets from each other. Sara was grateful for the support she had received from them after Scott died. They were like sisters to her. After her father had passed away a few years ago, she had no close relatives left.

"Brace yourselves. I'm changing the subject, ladies." Sara sipped her pomegranate martini. Brianne had made an entire pitcher for the group, although she was abstaining.

"We're listening," Tori said.

"I had a weird trip to the bank this morning. Apparently, Scott had an account in his own name and was transferring money to a bank account in Champaign each month. I've tried to call Jeremy, but I keep getting voice mail. This must have something to do with Jameson Family Entertainment."

"How much money every month? Are you sure Scott never mentioned it?" Brianne nibbled at a truffle.

"Two thousand a month. I don't think he mentioned it. But, hell, after Jack was born it was so hectic, and I was barely sleeping. I guess he could have mentioned it and I just don't remember." Sara's brow knitted as she tried to remember if Scott had ever mentioned anything.

She hated to admit she sometimes ignored talk about business when she was busy with Jack.

Tori shrugged. "It was probably expense money for when he traveled and wined and dined people. Wasn't he on the road about twenty days a month? That's a lot of airline and food expense."

"Yeah, in fact, when you think about it that way, two thousand isn't all that much. He probably ate out three meals a day for three-quarters of the month with several people as his guest. It's just strange. It makes me realize that there were times I may not have listened closely to what Scott was telling me. What other little things did I not know? Are there suits at some dry cleaner that I don't know about? Did he have library books on hold?" Sara blinked back a few tears.

Tori grabbed her hand. "Stop this shit. Stop it right now. I've been there, and it doesn't lead to anything good. Don't think about the times you lost your temper or didn't have time to hear about his day. We're human, dammit. Scott loved you, and you loved him. You both did the best you could. Scott wouldn't want you to do this to yourself, you know? He would want you to be happy and be a good mom to Jack."

Sara sniffed. "I know, I know. I just…it's just that he's been gone for over a year now. Shit! This is going to sound horrible. I'm a horrible person. Scott wasn't home much, so when he died…"

The women waited quietly for Sara to find the words. Saying them was going to sound awful.

"I got used to him being gone really quickly. Fuck, the last six months I've been so busy with Jack I've barely noticed that Scott's not there. Sometimes I would go days and not think about him. Now, I can go a week and not think about him. Isn't that a shitty thing to do? He was my husband and Jack's father, and I don't think about him all the time like I should."

There, she'd said it out loud. Hot tears trickled down Sara's face. Tori was the first to speak.

"You are not a horrible person, Sara. That's what is supposed to happen. Listen to me, because I've been there and I know of what I speak. You are alive. You're supposed to live your life and not dwell on Scott's memory every day. Of course, there will be times when you think about him more than others—birthdays, holidays, for instance. But we are meant to move on with our lives. It's our survival instinct on steroids. You're young and beautiful with a long life ahead of you. Scott would want you to live that life."

Lisa's eyes were sympathetic. "You're most certainly not a terrible person." The others nodded in agreement. "I think this means you're healing. You loved Scott, and a part of you always will. He's Jack's father. But your spirit is healing and is ready to move on. Live your life, Sara. It's the only one you get. It would be a sin to waste it, don't you think?"

Sara knew that was true. If Scott had known how little time he had, perhaps he might have lived life differently. She would be foolish to throw away her own life. When she looked at Jack, she knew she had been placed on this earth for a purpose. He deserved the best mother she could be. A happy, whole mother would be the right thing for him.

Noelle pushed the box of chocolates toward Sara. "Why don't you go to Champaign? Visit where Scott grew up. Get some kind of closure for yourself. You can spend some time with Scott's brother and his husband while you're there. Haven't they been begging you to visit for months?"

Brianne smiled. "That's a great idea! Jeremy and Cole have been asking you to come for a visit. They would love to see Jack."

That was true. Jeremy and Cole asked her practically every week to come up for a visit. They had come down at the holidays, and Jack had been in heaven. He loved his uncles dearly.

"You know, I think I will. School's out, and I don't have to be back until August. I can attend the book meetings by Skype." Sara brushed her tears with the back of her hand.

"Gotta love technology." Tori laughed. "You can read smutty stories with us a thousand miles away. Here's to your trip to Champaign." They all raised their glasses. For the first time in a long time, Sara was looking forward to something.

Chapter 2

Jeremy pushed his front door open and dropped his briefcase on the bench in the foyer. It had been a long fucking day. He was tired and still had a mountain of paperwork to look at before he could retire for the night. He also needed to return Sara's phone call. She had left him a voice mail earlier in the day, but he had yet to have a chance to return her call.

"There's my favorite executive." Cole came down the stairs and gave him a brief kiss. Jeremy's body tightened in response. He was amazed after all these years together he could still react to Cole like a horny teenage boy.

"You're my favorite creative pain in the ass." Jeremy nipped at Cole's bottom lip before taking possession of his lips again. Their tongues rubbed against each other in play. Jeremy tore his mouth away with a groan.

"Dinner first, fuck later." He'd missed lunch, and his stomach was growling at the amazing aroma wafting from the kitchen. It smelled like tomato sauce.

Cole chuckled. "The lasagna won't be ready for another forty-five minutes. I got sidetracked today. Sara called."

"Yeah, she called me, too, but I was in meetings all day. I'm glad you talked to her. Is everything all right?"

Jeremy's chest tightened with worry. Although Sara had good friends in Florida, she had no family to help her. She was basically a single, working parent with an active toddler. They talked to her each Sunday over Skype, and every week Jeremy could see the shadows under her eyes, even on the webcam. She needed someone to be there for her all the time. He had also seen her become stronger and more confident these last months. She was coming out of mourning and living fully. It was beautiful to see.

He, too, still mourned the passing of his little brother. Scott had been the charmer of the family. Everyone had loved him. It had been no surprise when Scott had married an amazing woman like Sara.

Cole's eyes twinkled. "She and Jack are coming for a visit. They'll be here on Saturday. I spent the day getting their bedrooms ready. Hope you don't mind, boss. The storyboard for the new game may take a day or two longer than I thought."

Jeremy barely registered Cole's assessment of their new project. He only heard one thing—Sara and Jack were coming. He smiled. It was about damn time.

"That's great. How long are they staying?" He would need to take some vacation so he could spend time with them.

"I talked her into an undetermined period of time. She was thinking a week, but I squashed that and convinced her to leave it open-ended. She's got the whole summer off from teaching. It would be great if we could convince her to stay the entire time or even longer."

Jeremy felt his grin getting wider. "We'll work on that."

Jeremy felt Cole's hand wander down his belly and cup his crotch. His cock hardened under Cole's practiced hand.

"You seem pretty happy with the news. It wouldn't have anything to do with how attractive you think Sara is, would it? How gorgeous we both think she is? How sweet she is, smart, and a great mother?"

Cole's deft fingers had his pants unbuttoned and his zipper down. Jeremy's cock sprang free into Cole's waiting hand.

"Fuck. That feels good." Jeremy panted as Cole massaged him from root to tip.

"We both think she's beautiful. Oh, fuck, like that..." Jeremy groaned as his balls pulled up. "But fuck, she's my brother's wife, for God's sake. You don't come on to your brother's wife."

Cole's hand slowed to torture speed.

"No, she *was* your brother's wife. Now she's a beautiful, young widow. I'm not saying we should come on to her. But there's nothing wrong with fantasizing a little. What would you do if she were here?"

Cole's hand reached down to cup his balls. "Would you want her to suck your cock? Or fuck her pussy? I'd want to eat her out. I bet her pussy tastes so good, don't you?"

Jeremy mashed his body against Cole's. "I need you, baby."

Cole dropped to his knees and gave Jeremy's cock a lick. He shook with arousal, pleasure suffusing his body. Cole gave the best blow jobs on the planet. His body was familiar with Cole's mouth and tongue and was already anticipating pleasure.

"I bet her hot little mouth would feel good on your cock. She could suck your dick while I fuck her from behind. Or she could ride you while she sucks me? My favorite fantasy is when we both take her together, me in her hot cunt and you in her tight ass."

Cole mercifully swallowed Jeremy's cock down. Jeremy was on the edge from Cole's words. It had always been Jeremy's dirty little secret that he desired his brother's wife. Cole, too. She had fueled more than a few lustful thoughts between the two of them. He and Cole loved each other, but they liked women, too. Jeremy had always wondered what might have happened if he had met Sara first. He felt a little guilty at the thoughts he'd had about her.

Cole's hot mouth moved up and down his rock-hard shaft. He wouldn't last long if Cole kept this up. His balls were painfully tight, and the pressure was building. His fingers tightened in Cole's hair, urging him on. He tightened his lips and gave a hum that sent vibrations through Jeremy's cock and balls. It was all he needed to send him over. He shoved his cock into the back of Cole's throat, holding it there while his hot cum filled his lover's mouth. His dick jerked and cum seemed to shoot forever before it was over. Cole licked him clean and tucked him back into his pants. Jeremy heaved a sigh.

"You look like you needed that, J." Cole stood and pulled him close.

"I did, but I don't want to leave you hanging."

Cole laughed. "You won't. Assume the position, baby."

Jeremy chuckled as he shucked his pants and shirt as he headed to their bedroom upstairs. They had been together several years and were comfortable being both top and bottom. He looked back and Cole was doing the same.

He would never get tired of looking at Cole's body. He was blond, just like himself. But where Jeremy's eyes were blue, Cole's were a soft golden brown. His body was strong and muscular, with a wide chest and flat abs. Cole's impressive cock jutted out from a thatch of blond hair, ready for action. Jeremy reached out to caress it.

"This for me? I'm not sure I can take all of this." Jeremy smirked.

Cole grinned at Jeremy's playfulness. "Really? You've been taking it several times a week for about ten years now. You're about to take it now, too. How do you want it?"

It was always a battle in the bedroom between them. They were both dominant men, and being submissive every now and then was something they compromised on. Jeremy gave up the control tonight.

"Your choice, baby."

"Then I'll take you spoon position." Cole grabbed the lube from the bedside table. Jeremy got into position on his left side and felt the first trickles of lube run down his ass crack. Despite blowing his wad just minutes before, his cock was already reinflating at the dirty thoughts he was having. Thoughts centered around him, Sara, and Cole and some raunchy, dirty sex.

Cole lined up his cock with Jeremy's back hole. He could feel the brush of hair on his legs and smell Cole's spicy scent. Cole didn't wear any cologne. He didn't need to. He smelled amazing just from soap and water.

Jeremy rocked his hips to let Cole know he was ready, hell, anxious to be nailed. Cole took the hint and thrust hard into his ass all the way to the hilt. Jeremy felt Cole's balls slap his ass and the crinkle of pubic hair against his skin. He hissed at the burn that quickly morphed into pleasure. Cole held still. Waiting.

"Fuck me. Hard."

It was all Cole needed. He started slowly at first, riding Jeremy's ass, his cock sending shivers of pleasure up Jeremy's spine. He built up speed until he was slamming into Jeremy's ass. Jeremy pushed back with each stroke, a full and willing participant. Their breathing came in bursts and pants, their bodies slick with sweat. Jeremy felt Cole's hand reach around and fist his swollen cock.

"Come with me, baby. I love you so much."

Cole picked up speed with his cock and his hand. Jeremy felt his climax build in his balls and fire from his cock. Ropes of cum shot out and painted the sheets and Cole's hand. He felt his ass clamp down on Cole's cock. Cole thrust in once more and froze, gripping his hip tightly. Jeremy could feel Cole's hot cum filling his hole before they both fell back against the pillows.

Jeremy lifted Cole's fingers to his lips and kissed them tenderly. He had spent the last decade with this man, and God willing he would spend many more. "I love you, too, baby. I doubt you know how much."

Cole gave him a cocky grin. "Oh, I think I might have an idea. Let's get cleaned up and have dinner. We have a lot of plans to make before Sara and Jack get here."

Jeremy grinned back. It would be wonderful having them here. If only he could convince them to stay.

* * * *

Cole spotted Sara as she exited the plane. She had Jack on her hip and a diaper bag on her shoulder. As always, he was struck by her beauty. She was tiny in stature but curvy in all the right places. Her features were delicate, her lips full and sensuous, and her eyes a sparkling green. Her hair was dark and sleek, hanging down to the middle of her back. Unlike many new mothers, Sara had never given in to the urge to cut it for simplicity.

Those green eyes were now scanning the crowded airport looking for a familiar face. He raised his arm and waved. Her eyes locked with his, and he felt a jolt of awareness through his body. He ignored the now-familiar feeling and rushed forward to wrap his arms around them both. Sara's body felt warm and soft against his.

"Missed you, princess," he whispered in the shell of her ear. Her scent wafted over him. It was something softly floral yet slightly exotic.

She pulled back and shook her head with a smile. "Only you and Jeremy call me 'princess.'"

Cole reached for Jack, lifting him and twirling him around to the child's delight. "I'm writing a new game, and I'm going to make a princess that looks just like you."

Sara pulled a face. "I suppose you'll have a prince that has to save her? Can't you make me a princess that kicks butt?"

"Butt!" Jack crowed.

Sara gave him a weary look. "I never learn. Just to warn you, he's a parrot these days. Anything you say, he's going to say, too. Especially if you don't want him to."

"Consider me warned. I'm going to teach him to say Uncle Cole and Uncle Jeremy. Oh, and I'm going to teach him to say that he wants to stay here and never leave."

Sara hitched the diaper bag higher on her shoulder. "You say that now. Wait until you have an energetic toddler ripping your house apart. The crumbs alone will make you crazy."

Cole cuddled Jack closer and grabbed the diaper bag from Sara and threw it over his shoulder. He was secure enough in his manhood to carry a diaper bag.

"I'll take the chance. I have a DustBuster. But we don't have you or Jack. C'mon, let's get your suitcases and get on the road. It will only take about an hour and a half to drive to Champaign from Indianapolis."

Cole felt a deep satisfaction now that Sara and Jack were here. He would see to it that Sara got some rest and relaxation. She deserved it.

Chapter 3

Sara held on to Jack's hand as they walked up the long driveway. Jeremy and Cole's home in Mahomet, a small bedroom community outside of Champaign, was impressive. The two-story home sat on a large wooded lot. The front porch alone was larger than Sara's first apartment in South Tampa.

Cole unlocked the front door and ushered her through the entryway. Jack tugged his hand free of Sara's, and he went running to explore. She started after him, but Cole's warm hand on her shoulder stayed her.

"Don't worry. I toddler-proofed the whole house. There isn't anything breakable under three feet, and all the outlets have covers. Jeremy even put gates at the top and the bottom of the stairs and cabinet locks all over the house."

Sara hugged Cole in gratitude. So many people didn't understand the chaos a toddler could wreak on a home. She was surprised when Cole hugged her back, running his hand up and down her spine. Tingles of pleasure ran through her body. It had been a long time since anyone had touched her other than Jack. She loved his grimy hugs but missed having strong arms hold her.

"You'll probably want to freshen up from traveling. Let me show you your rooms."

Cole grabbed the diaper bag and scooped up Jack before bounding up the stairs. She envied his energy. Lately, she felt like she was running on an empty tank. She could probably curl up and sleep for a week.

Sara knew the way to the guest room where they would be staying. She pushed the door open and gasped in surprise. It was now a toddler's dream bedroom. Jack was wriggling in Cole's arms wanting to be let down.

Cole put him gently on the floor. "What do you think, princess? I can tell Jack likes it."

Sara was still in shock. The room was decorated entirely in DC Comics superheroes, including Jack's favorite, the Green Lantern. Jack was bounding around the room rubbing at the walls which were covered in colorful transfers and then running to the myriad of toys stacked on low shelves along one wall.

"Holy shit," Sara whispered softly.

Cole gave her a wide grin. "I'll take that as a 'Wow, I love it.'"

He pushed open the closet. "I put away his clothes, and yours, too, in the other room. They arrived this morning."

Cole had convinced her to send most of their clothes and Jack's toys ahead by UPS. That way she wouldn't be wrestling with suitcases, a diaper bag, and Jack through airports. It had turned out to be a great idea.

Sara plopped into a tiny chair that sat next to a tiny table full of art supplies. She was overwhelmed.

"How…when did you do all this? I just called on Wednesday."

"It wasn't easy, but I had the bones of the work already done. The furniture and bedding were already here. I just needed to make the final touches. I asked a friend of mine to help, in all honesty. She's a decorator and had a great time with it."

Sara grabbed Cole's hand. "I don't know what to say, Cole. This is so over the top and so just like you. Thank you."

Everything Cole did was over the top. He was a creative genius who saw things in a way that no one else could see them. She never would have been able to pull a room together like this. She doubted he really needed the designer's help.

"Ready to see your room?"

Cole tugged her from the chair. Jack was happily playing with a puzzle he had pulled from one of the shelves.

"C'mon, he'll be fine in here. I locked the gate to the stairs."

Sara let Cole drag her to the next room. She vaguely remembered this room as Jeremy's office. It wasn't an office anymore. Sara couldn't hold back her sigh of pleasure as she ran her hand over the light blue and chocolate-brown satin bedspread. The walls were also light blue with heavy chocolate-colored drapes and blue flower embellishments. The bed was a huge four-poster in dark and light woods. There was a rocking chair by the window and a tall, old-fashioned full-length mirror by the door that led to the bathroom.

Sara knew her expression was stunned.

"Wasn't this Jeremy's office?"

Cole shook his head. "We moved Jeremy's office downstairs last year after the renovations to the backyard were complete. Now Jeremy can look out his office window at the new landscaping. I give all the credit for this bedroom to my friend. Honestly, I didn't know what a woman would like."

Sara trailed her fingers down the bedpost. "It's beautiful. Your friend is very talented. I don't know what to say, Cole. 'Thank you' seems so inadequate. Why did you go to all this trouble?"

Cole crossed his arms over his broad chest and gave her an arrogant look.

"Why wouldn't we go to this trouble, princess? You're fucking family. Besides, we want you to feel like this is your home while you're here. As a matter of fact, we want you to feel like this is your home. Period. I'll wait until Jeremy gets home to discuss this further, but we want you to move here permanently."

Sara was speechless. Yes, the men had often made that offer, but she never thought they were serious. She thought they were just being nice and polite.

"Seriously, Cole? My friends are in Florida, my job. I can't just pick up my life and move here on a whim."

"It would hardly be a whim. They have teaching jobs up here, though you wouldn't need to work. You don't need to work now. And we're family, aren't we? Don't answer right now. Why don't you rest up from your trip? I'll watch Jack. Just relax, princess, have a soak in the tub or a nap. We're here to help you."

Sara started to protest. "Jack needs a new—"

Cole put his finger over her lips. "I can change a diaper, Sara. I'll get him a snack, too. You relax. That's a fucking order."

Cole turned and walked out of the room, gently shutting the door behind him. Sara looked helplessly around the gorgeous room. For the first time in almost two years, she had nothing to do.

* * * *

Jeremy walked into controlled chaos. Toys were everywhere. Jack was riding Cole around the living room piggyback while the television blared in the background what Jeremy supposed was some sort of educational show for children. It looked deadly dull. Thank goodness he had stopped at Target and picked up the Scooby-Doo DVDs on his way home from the office. No way was he going to watch Barney or Teletubbies.

Cole stopped in front of him and turned so Jeremy could take Jack. "Say hi to Uncle Jeremy, Jack."

"Hi, J." Jack gave him a grin, showing off teeth that hadn't been there at Christmas.

"J? Gee, I wonder who taught him that?" Jeremy hugged Jack's little body close. He had missed the little guy.

"Well, 'Jeremy' is quite a mouthful for a toddler to say." Cole smirked.

"I hope I'm more than a mouthful," Jeremy said under his breath.

"I heard that."

"Luckily, Jack didn't." Jack was busy pulling at his expensive silk tie. He'd had a business meeting that morning. He was trying to clear his schedule as much as possible to spend time with Sara and Jack.

"Where's Sara?" Even not seeing her yet, Jeremy felt the pull toward her. He could swear he smelled her perfume in the house. Jeremy set Jack down on the floor and watched him scamper to his toys.

"Upstairs. I gave her an order to rest. I told her I could handle Jack."

Jeremy quirked an eyebrow. "And how did our princess take to being ordered around?"

Cole laughed. "Surprisingly well. If I didn't know better, I would think she liked it."

"We know better." He and Cole had more than once witnessed Sara telling Scott not to try that caveman shit with her. It had only made him admire her more, if that was possible.

"Do you want a shower before we head to dinner?"

Jeremy stretched. "Yeah, I could use a quick shower. Where are we going, or do I even need to ask?"

"Monical's Pizza, baby. Sara loves it, you know."

Jeremy took the stairs two at a time, laughing. "And what Sara wants, Sara gets."

* * * *

Sara pushed away her plate. She was officially stuffed. When Jeremy had returned home from work, he and Cole had loaded her and Jack into their SUV and taken them to Monical's for pizza. Sara loved the thin-crust pizza, cut into squares. She could only get it when she and Scott visited his family. It was certainly a treat for her first night in town.

Jack had eaten some pizza and a breadstick with cheese dipping sauce. He was sitting on Cole's lap while Jeremy wiped his face and hands. She felt like a queen. Jeremy and Cole had barely let her lift a finger since arriving.

"Jeremy, I had a meeting at the bank earlier this week. It's one of the reasons I came up here."

Jeremy looked up from cleaning Jack's face. His expression was concerned.

"Is everything okay? Do you need money, princess? I told you when Scott died that you didn't need to work. The business makes more than enough money to support you and Jack. It was part Scott's, and now his part belongs to you."

Sara laid her hand on his arm. He was so sweet to be concerned, but she could take care of herself. "No, everything is fine. I have my salary from teaching, the life insurance proceeds, and the quarterly allowance you send me from the business. I don't have any money worries. This was about an account that Scott was sending money to. He sent two thousand dollars a month to an account here in Champaign. I assume it has something to do with the business since we aren't short any money. The only reason I found out is that the account he transferred the money from went to a zero balance. I went ahead and authorized the transfer from my own account for this month."

Jeremy frowned. "An account here in Champaign? I'm not aware of any account." He looked at Cole. "Do you know anything about this?"

Cole shrugged. "I'm creative, not an accountant. Check with Steve on Monday. He'll know. Maybe he and Scott were doing something with expenses and he forgot to stop the transfers. It's probably no big deal."

Sara was puzzled. She had assumed that Jeremy knew all about it. "You don't know anything about it? Isn't that strange? Do I need to be concerned?"

Jeremy smiled reassuringly. "Not all that strange. I don't get involved with every single bank account we have. I'll get the details on Monday from Steve. Do you have the account number?"

Sara pulled a card from her purse. "This is it. You'll find out?"

"Of course. I'll talk to Steve when he gets back from vacation. I just remembered he left for a few weeks." Jeremy tucked the card in his pocket and reached for Jack.

Sara sighed. "You're spoiling him. He's going to want to be held every minute when we go home. As it is, I feel like I do everything with one hand. I cook, clean, read, even talk on the phone with him on my hip."

"We don't want you to go home. I know Cole mentioned it. We want you to stay here with us. We miss you and we miss Jack. We can help you. You do too much on your own. And speaking of carrying him on your hip, we made a massage appointment for you on Monday."

Sara was torn between gratitude—her back ached constantly—or being pissed off at their high-handedness. She tried to walk the line between the two.

"I appreciate that, Jeremy. My back does take a beating. However"—she gave them a stern schoolteacher look—"I'm not sure that I'm up for discussing pulling up stakes and moving our lives here. I have a life in Florida. Yes, it's been hard. But it's. My. Life."

They both had the grace to look ashamed. Cole stroked her arm. "We're sorry, princess. We're just so damned glad to have you here. We swear we're not trying to take over your life. We just want to take care of you, pamper you a little. Is that so bad?"

No, it wasn't bad. It was wonderful. Fabulous. Scott hadn't been the pampering type. He preferred to be pampered, if the truth be known. She had never minded. She loved taking care of him and making him feel special and loved. He had always shown appreciation for all she did.

But these men in one night had made her feel more relaxed and cared for than she could ever remember being. It didn't help that she was acutely aware of them. They were both incredibly handsome, incredibly male. Their hard bodies drew her eye wherever they were in the house. They smelled amazing, too. Both smelled manly but different. Jeremy had a woodsy scent, while Cole's was spicier. She could breathe them in all night. She was embarrassed that her panties had gone quite damp when she was around them. She prayed they couldn't smell her arousal.

That would be beyond humiliating. Cole and Jeremy had been so good to her. She wouldn't repay their kindness by embarrassing them with her out-of-control libido. She blamed this on being without a man for so long. Now she had two, one on each side, and her touch-starved body was begging for attention.

"No, it isn't bad. I'm just not used to it, that's all."

Jeremy leaned back in his chair and crossed his arms over his broad chest. His biceps strained against the short sleeves of his T-shirt.

"Get used to it, princess. We've only just begun."

Chapter 4

Sara padded the short distance down the hall to Jack's bedroom. She wanted to check on him one more time before she turned in. His first night in an unfamiliar place could make for an eventful sleep. Luckily, he had been so exhausted from traveling and the excitement, he had fallen asleep easily. Jack was a heavy sleeper. With any luck, he would sleep the night through. She peeked into his room and gazed at his angelic face. Her heart ached that he would grow up without a father's love. It just wasn't fair. Jack would be without a father's love and she would be without a man's love. Yes, they had each other, but it really wasn't the same.

She couldn't help but think about the conversation at the book club. She did owe it to Jack and Scott to live her life to the fullest, not wasting a moment. She deserved to be happy. She was a good mom and had been a good wife. Her heart was lonely and her body craved physical contact. That much was clear. One evening with Jeremy and Cole and she was thinking naughty thoughts that left her panties damp and her skin flushed.

She had always found them handsome and sexy, but tonight her desire was in overdrive. She couldn't help but notice the secret smiles between them, the comfortable and loving vibe they gave off, or the way they accidentally brushed against each other. They appeared to be happily in love.

She blew a kiss to Jack and stepped into the hall, stopping at a strange noise. She stayed very still, listening for it again. Her first night in a strange home was sure to have unfamiliar noises she would have to get used to. She heard it again and felt her face get warm. The noise she was hearing was moaning and groaning. Jeremy and Cole must be making love.

As if she couldn't control her own legs, she found herself standing outside their bedroom door. She could hear their muffled voices.

"Fuck me, J. Fuck me hard. God, I love you."

"I love you, too, baby. I'm going to fuck you and then I'm going to suck you dry. I love your cock. You're going to give me a mouthful of cum."

"Yes, I'm going to fuck your mouth, hard and fast."

Sara gasped at her own arousal from the nasty, dirty talk. Her nipples were hard against her T-shirt, and honey had soaked her panties and dampened her pajama shorts. Her breath was coming in pants. She fled back to the sanctuary of her bedroom, heart pounding, hoping that they hadn't seen or heard her.

She jumped into bed and pulled the covers over her, lying very still, waiting for a sign that she had been caught. As the minutes passed, she slowly relaxed, her heart rate returning to normal. That was really stupid. She should be ashamed of herself, listening in to their intimate moments.

That's how low you've sunk.

Sara closed her eyes in shame. She would have to pay close attention to how they acted in the morning to see if she had been found out.

* * * *

Cole pressed against Jeremy's back.

"Morning, handsome. Sleep well?"

Jeremy turned from the pancakes he was making and grinned.

"Excellent. Someone wore me out."

"The pleasure was all mine." Cole smirked.

"I think it was mutual."

Cole looked toward the stairs. "Princess awake yet?"

Jeremy shook his head. "Nope. I hope she sleeps in today. I got Jack out of bed, and he's working on breakfast."

Jeremy waved a spatula to where Jack was eating a pancake with his bare hands and making quite a mess at the kitchen table.

Cole leaned over and gave Jack's sticky cheek a kiss.

"Morning, sunshine. Like pancakes?"

"Me eat pa-cakes." Jack chortled with a grin.

"I think I need a stack myself. Want some more milk, Jack?"

"Milk. More!" Jack banged his empty sippy cup on the table.

Cole grabbed it and started to refill it.

"Say please, Jack."

Jack showed off his new teeth. "Peez!"

"Here you go. You're welcome, buddy."

Cole turned back to Jeremy.

"Do you think she knows we know?" Cole's voice was low.

"Are you sure we know? That noise outside our bedroom may not have been Sara listening. Maybe it was our imagination."

Cole shook his head. "No way. I know what I heard. It was her. She was listening to us making love. Fuck, I wish she had just opened the door and joined us. My cock's hard just thinking about it."

Jeremy's smile was rueful. "Me, too. But Sara isn't the kind of woman who gets off an airplane, has some pizza, and then jumps into bed with two men. No matter what kind of *Penthouse* fantasies we have."

Cole grinned. "Let's leave the door propped open. Just in case."

* * * *

"Tina, I know Steve's on vacation, but can you check on one of our bank accounts for me? I need to know what it's for."

Jeremy handed the card Sara had given him to Steve's assistant. He hoped Tina could tell him about the account. He had to admit that he was curious as to why his little brother was sending two thousand dollars to a bank account here in Champaign.

"I can try, boss. I don't have Steve's level of access, though."

Jeremy leaned against the file cabinet while Tina's fingers flew over the keyboard. Long moments later she handed him the card back, shaking her head.

"I can't find that account in our database. But if it's one of our bank accounts, perhaps I just don't have access. You own the joint, though. You should have access."

Tina gave him a teasing smile. Jeremy laughed.

"True. If I sign in, can you execute the query? You know I hate this accounting stuff."

Tina grinned. "Yeah, I know. You'd rather be writing a new video game. I get it. Yeah, just sign in here."

Jeremy leaned down and typed his credentials into the computer. He loved computers, but he hated talking debit and credits. He could get into talking about the financials of the company but didn't want to delve into the details of every transaction for copy paper and pens.

Tina pressed a few buttons and shook her head again.

"Sorry, boss. There's no account number that matches. Is this some super-secret slush fund for executives?"

"Ha-ha, I wish. I guess I'll wait until Steve comes back and see if he knows anything about it."

"Probably your best bet. Maybe it's a new account and he hasn't added it yet."

Jeremy could only hope so. If not, he had serious questions as to what Scott had been up to.

* * * *

Sara leaned back in the chaise lounge and watched Cole and Jack finger painting. Cole came home early from work and insisted they all sit on the verandah and paint. Sara finger painted a picture of the rising sun and was now sipping on iced tea. Cole and Jack were turning out masterpiece after masterpiece. No way would there be room enough on the refrigerator for all these pictures.

The last two weeks had been some of the most restful and relaxing that Sara could remember. Having both Jeremy and Cole around to help her with Jack had taken such a burden from her shoulders. Jack, too, had blossomed under all the male attention he was receiving. Sara felt slightly guilty she hadn't brought him to visit sooner. He needed strong, positive male role models. Jeremy and Cole certainly fit the bill.

There had also been no mention of the evening that Sara had overheard them making love. Thank goodness they hadn't heard her in the hall. That would have been embarrassing beyond belief. As it was, she fought the images in her brain every night when she closed her eyes. Her dreams were filled with their strong hands and mouths stroking and kissing her body. She woke up with soaked panties every morning.

"My do." Jack pulled the paint jar out of Cole's hand. Lately, everything was Jack's "to do." Since coming here, Jack's confidence had skyrocketed and he wanted to do everything himself.

"Not this time, buddy. Let Uncle Cole pour out the paint." Cole quickly poured the paint and placed Jack's hands in the squishy medium before a tantrum could start.

Cole turned and gave her a smile. She felt her heart flip-flop and her stomach flutter. It happened every time she was with one or both of these men. It wasn't just that they were handsome or sexy, although they were. In spades. They were fine men. They worked hard. But they balanced work with a sense of friends and family. Sara never got the idea from them that work was their number-one priority.

Sara smiled back. "Tantrum nicely averted. You know it won't always be that way, right? Sometimes you can do everything right, but he'll be tired or hungry and we can't do anything to console him."

Cole wiped his paint-covered hands on a towel and plopped at the end of the lounge chair.

"I'm just glad when it works. I know there will be times we have to say no to him for his own good and he's not going to like it one little bit. I'm guessing we'll hear about it. He seems to have pretty healthy lungs on him."

Indeed he did. Jeremy and Cole had learned just how healthy a few days before when Sara wouldn't let Jack have a second cookie. He was one upset little boy.

Cole snagged his iced tea glass and took a gulp. "I've been thinking about his birthday party. Why don't we have a cookout here at the house? It's the Fourth of July, too. We can have a double celebration."

"A cookout? It's great weather for it, but I don't want you to go to any trouble. Jack's only going to be two. He won't remember a party. We can just take him for pizza and to the park. I went shopping yesterday and bought him some new toys. That's what he'll really care about." Sara chuckled.

"Will you stop acting like you're this giant imposition? We love having you here. Let me repeat that. We love having you here. We don't want you to leave. A cookout is no big deal. We love to have people over, and this is a great excuse."

Sara rolled her eyes. "Got it. No imposition. Love having me here. Check. Okay, it sounds like a great idea. What can I do?"

Cole ran his finger down her bare arm, making her skin tingle and her pussy cream. His scent surrounded her, mixing with the outdoors. It was heady stuff. "We'll start planning after dinner. Casual, but great food. Kid-friendly food. How does that sound, princess?"

"Great. Terrific." Even to her own ears, she sounded breathless.

Cole looked at her with his soulful brown eyes. "You like being here, right, princess? We're making you happy?"

Sara squeezed his hand. "Yes. I'm having a great time. I haven't been this rested since before Jack was born. It's been wonderful."

Cole lifted her fingers to his lips, kissing them tenderly.

"I'm glad. We want you to be very, very happy here. Let us know if there's anything else we can do."

How about make love to me?

Sara shook her head to pull herself out of the daze his mesmerizing gaze had put her in. "Nothing else. There's nothing else."

Cole quirked an eyebrow. "If you're sure, princess."

* * * *

Sara leaned back in the bathtub, replaying the conversation with Cole. It had almost seemed as if he was flirting with her. That couldn't be the case, of course. Jeremy and Cole were a couple. They had been together, happily, for years.

They were probably just being kind, realizing she hadn't had much male attention in the last months. Sara sighed as she thought of Scott. He had literally swept her off her feet. He had been on vacation in Florida when they met at a beachside restaurant. When he returned to Illinois after his one-week vacation, she thought she'd never see him again. How wrong she was. He had e-mailed her the minute he arrived home. Six months and six visits later, Scott had proposed. They had decided to make Florida their home due to the poor health of Sara's father.

She had never regretted marrying Scott. Their marriage had been a happy one. No relationship was perfect, but they worked at it. It had been difficult with Scott gone so often, traveling for business, but it was worth it.

Was she disloyal for being attracted to Jeremy and Cole? Scott had probably found other women attractive when they were married. It was only natural. She stared at the ring finger of her left hand. She had stopped wearing her ring shortly after Scott died. She was constantly taking it off anyway to change diapers so one day she just never put it back on.

She wasn't married anymore. The girls had reminded her to embrace life and not waste a moment. Surely there was nothing wrong with panting after these two men? They were so hunky and sexy, any card-carrying woman would be aroused.

She simply needed to make sure that they never found out how attractive she thought they were. She sunk farther into the water until it lapped at her chin. Yep, that was what she needed to do. Just play it cool and act like she wasn't in heat every time she was close to them. Piece of fucking cake.

Chapter 5

Jeremy held Sara's hand as they walked down Green Street past the shops and onto Wright Street. The casual visitor to Champaign-Urbana would never realize that Wright Street was the dividing line between the twin cities, so seamlessly they had grown together. He tugged her hand and led her toward the north quad of the university. Red-brick, ivy-covered buildings flanked the quad on all sides. Both he and Scott were alumni of the University of Illinois. Born and raised in Urbana, Illinois, they often joked they bled orange and blue.

Sara had been quiet most of the day. Her request to tour the campus had come as a surprise, but Jeremy had been happy to grant it. He chuckled as he remembered some of the hijinks from his college days.

"I heard that laugh, Jeremy. What are you remembering?"

Jeremy shook his head firmly. "You'll never get it out of me, Sara. The past is best left in the past. But I have fond memories of it."

Sara's expression turned serious. "Yes, the past is best left in the past."

She turned to him. "Thank you for bringing me here. Part of this trip is to make peace with Scott's passing. I wanted to see where he went to school. He spoke of it often, unlike you, but somehow he never brought me here to see it when we visited."

Jeremy slipped his arms around Sara's petite frame, breathing in her tantalizing fragrance. She looked up in surprise but gripped his arms.

"I'm sure he meant to, princess. Scott loved his college years. How else do you want to make peace? I'm all for that."

Sara's lower lip trembled, and her eyes were bright with unshed tears. "I don't think about him every day. My friends say that means my heart is healing. I thought if I came up here I would think about him all the time. But, I don't."

He tightened his embrace. "Don't feel guilty, Sara. Scott wouldn't want that from you. He would want you to move on and live your life. Scott wouldn't want you to waste the time you have in this life. No one knows how long they have left. We have to live every day to the fullest."

Jeremy believed every word he said. When Scott had died, Jeremy had visited the doctor to make sure his own heart was healthy. It was, but he wouldn't take any day for granted.

A single tear slid down her satiny cheek, and she gave him a slight smile. "You sound like my friends. I want to live every day. Not just for me, but for Jack, too. He deserves a happy mom. I want to give him everything. I think I've held on to the grief inside me for so long, if I give it up, I'll be so empty, Jeremy. What will take its place?"

Jeremy brushed at the tear on her cheek. "Love, Sara. Fill it up with lots of love."

It was then and there Jeremy vowed that he and Cole would fill her life with love. He, too, would let go of the grief he held for Scott and move on. He wanted to move on with this extraordinary woman. She was strong, brave, and full of love. She was everything to him and Cole.

He hugged her close, his heart bursting, and looked up at the heavens.

I love you, brother. But I've fallen in love with Sara, too. We always did have the same taste in women. I hope you're okay with Cole and I loving and caring for her and Jack. I'll make sure I tell him stories about you. He'll know about you, bro. We won't forget you.

He released his hold and tugged her hand. "There's only one way to go, Sara. Forward."

Sara gave him a smile. "You're right. Forward."

She lifted their entwined fingers. "Will you hold my hand? Forward is kind of scary."

He lifted her fingers to his lips and kissed them tenderly. "I'll hold your hand forever, Sara. Both Cole and I will."

* * * *

His tongue circled her clit over and over, sending her into orbit. She grabbed his long hair and tugged his mouth closer, grinding her pussy onto his face.

"Lick me! Oh God, lick me!"

Steve licked her clit with the flat of his tongue while Stan sucked her turgid nipple into his hot mouth. His teeth scraped the sensitive flesh while his fingers plucked at the other nipple. She wiggled restlessly under their ministrations, moaning and groaning her pleasure.

"I need your cock. Please, somebody fuck me!"

Steve lifted his head from her drenched cunt. "We're going to fuck you, baby. My big cock in your swollen pussy and Stan's dick in your virgin ass. You're going to love it, baby. You haven't been fucked until you've been fucked by me and Stan. Now you're going to come for us."

Steve shoved two fingers inside her and lapped at her clit. Her body exploded with pleasure as she called their names.

Stan let go of her nipples and practically lifted her on top of Steve. He smacked her ass several times, sending her climbing toward another orgasm.

"Ride him, baby. I want to see you work for your next orgasm."

"I wouldn't mind having two men, but not these guys." Tori frowned. "They kind of seemed like assholes."

Sara laughed. "What I don't get is why all the men assume the woman is an ass virgin. I mean if these guys have all this experience, and the women are ass virgins, just who are these men fucking to get this experience? Is there one woman out there that teaches men what to do?"

She was attending the book club over Skype. Cole had even made her a cosmo and bought her a box of Godiva chocolates to enjoy during the meeting.

Lisa laughed at Sara's question. "You have a very good point there. Perhaps there's some secret ass-fucking class all men in a ménage need to take and pass before they can unleash their impressive cocks on unsuspecting ass virgins everywhere?"

The women fell into peals of laughter.

"Stop!" Brianne begged. "It's hard to laugh with this baby pressing on my ribs and bladder."

Brianne was eight months pregnant, and her husband, Nate, and son, Kade, were over the moon. Kade couldn't wait to have a brother or sister.

Brianne smiled at Sara through the webcam. "You seem very lighthearted today, Sar. We haven't seen you this happy and relaxed in a very long time. It's good to see you like this."

The other women nodded and agreed.

Noelle grinned. "What's your secret? Is Mahomet, Illinois, that fun and exciting? Should we all be booking tours?"

Sara laughed. "I don't know if I would call it exciting, but it is relaxing. The guys are just really wonderful, helping me with Jack. It's been…well, a move forward."

Lisa leaned into the camera to get a closer look at Sara's face. "Forward, huh? The way you said that word means something, girl. Time to spill the beans. What's going on there?"

Sara set her drink down and leaned into the camera, too. This was serious business, not their usual banter.

"You guys were right. I am healing. I'm moving forward and embracing life. I'm alive, and I want to feel that way. Jeremy and

Cole have been so supportive. I'm making peace with Scott's memory, and I'm ready to make some new ones."

It felt wonderful to say it aloud. She felt happy and strong and so alive. It was as if she could feel the blood coursing through her veins and her heart beating in her chest.

Tori spoke first, her voice thick with emotion. "That's great, honey. I'm so happy for you. You can't bring Scott back. You can only make the best life for you and Jack. This is a good day."

Brianne, Lisa, and Noelle cheered, "Go, Sara!"

Sara felt her face grow warm. If they only knew the "moving forward" thoughts she'd been having about Jeremy and Cole. Her fantasies had only grown stronger and more vivid, incorporating some of the things she had read in the book club over the years.

"Thanks for the support. It means a lot to me, you know. I don't think I could have made it through the last fifteen months without you. You're like sisters to me."

Lisa sniffed a little. "Don't fucking make me cry, Sara. I hate crying in front of others."

"Princess, Jeremy called. He wants us to meet him in Champaign for dinner."

Cole's voice pulled Sara from her X-rated thoughts only to plunge her into another set of X-rated thoughts. He popped his head into Jeremy's office quickly before disappearing just as quickly.

Brianne arched an eyebrow. "Yeah, *princess*. Jeremy wants to go to dinner."

Sara decided a good offense was the best defense. "You just wish you were a princess," she mocked.

Noelle rolled her eyes. "Remember Brianne's husband, Nate? He worships the ground she walks on, remember? Treats her like a goddess, so I think she's not jealous. I, on the other hand, am completely jealous. He was yummy. He's taken, huh?"

Sara nodded vigorously. She needed the reminder herself. "Very, very taken. Like totally taken. Both of them."

Noelle heaved a big sigh. "Too bad. That would be a ménage I wouldn't mind trying."

Sara could only bite her lip and silently agree.

* * * *

Sara tossed and turned. The day with Jeremy was so amazing and then the book club meeting. It had all been so emotional and yet freeing, too.

She had felt so close to Jeremy today. Holding his hand, surrounded by his scent, she had been overwhelmed with feelings. Yes, some of those feelings were sad ones. Saying good-bye to Scott was painful, but moving forward was exhilarating. She felt alive in a way she hadn't for so long, and all because of these two men.

She didn't want to be sad anymore. She wanted to live and be happy. She wanted to do exactly what Jeremy said—fill the now-empty space with love. There was only one problem. She wanted to move forward with them.

Sara turned over and punched her pillow. Jeremy and Cole were obviously very much in love. She had a snowball's chance in hell of being with them. But she could still fantasize, couldn't she? Lord knew they had starred in her dreams—both day and night—since coming here. They weren't just sexy and handsome, although they had those qualities by the bucketful. They were good men, too. They were so wonderful with Jack it almost brought tears to her eyes. They worked hard and would be good examples of fine men for her son. It was too bad she and Jack wouldn't be around them past the end of the summer.

Sara threw the covers back. She might as well go downstairs and make a cup of herbal tea. She wasn't going to get much sleep at this rate. She pushed open her bedroom door and stepped into the hallway. She couldn't stop her gaze from going straight to Jeremy and Cole's bedroom door. This night, it was partially open and a dim light emanated from it.

Her eyes widened and her face grew warm as she realized that there was noise coming from their room. Noise very much like the last time. Despite her mind yelling at her to stop, her feet walked toward their door. The sounds from the bedroom were obvious. Jeremy and Cole were making love. Her nipples peaked and rubbed against her tank top. Her pussy started dripping honey at the thought of their hard male bodies pressed against each other. Her mind altered the picture slightly and it was she sandwiched in between all that manly muscle.

She stopped in front of their door, closing her eyes and willing herself to retreat. This was none of her business. But the devil on her shoulder kept egging her on, telling her it was only a peek. They would never know. She opened her eyes slowly to a sight that took her breath away.

Jeremy and Cole were beautifully naked. Both looked like they had been sculpted from marble—wide chests, flat, defined abs, and muscled arms and legs. Her eyes drifted down to their cocks, and Sara couldn't stop from licking her lips at the thought of sucking them, feeling them slide past her lips and into her mouth. They were both large with Cole slightly beefier in girth while Jeremy was slightly longer. Either one would more than fill her drenched pussy, she was sure.

Cole was lying on his back with Jeremy leaning over him licking his nipples. Every time Jeremy nipped at them, Cole would moan and dig his fingers into Jeremy's biceps. It was the most erotic thing Sara had ever seen.

She must have made a noise because suddenly both men froze and turned toward her. She was poised to flee when they both smiled. She had expected anger and indignation at her invasion of their privacy, not acceptance.

Jeremy held out his hand to her. "Come, princess. Come join us."

His voice was husky with passion.

Cole beckoned to her. "We've been waiting for you, princess. Come join us. We want you so much."

She wanted them, too. More than she had ever wanted any man in her life. She moved toward the bed and their outstretched arms.

Chapter 6

Cole held his breath as Sara moved slowly toward them. He held very still, not making any sudden movement that might break the spell. He and Jeremy had been fantasizing about this moment for so long, and it was finally here. There was a part of him that was sure he was only dreaming.

But dreams didn't have a scent. Sara's soft, floral fragrance surrounded him, and the smell of her arousal made his already-hard cock throb with need. She wanted them. Her body couldn't lie. He could see the outline of her pebbled nipples through the thin cotton of her white tank top. She was definitely aroused.

He grabbed her hand and brought it to his lips. "We've been waiting for you, princess."

Jeremy held her other hand. "We want you, Sara. Do you want us? We've been dreaming about this for a very long time."

Sara's expression was one of passion, but her teeth were worrying her bottom lip. Something was holding her back. Cole pulled himself up and brushed a soft kiss over those lush lips and almost groaned at her sweet taste.

"What's wrong, princess? Don't you want us, too?"

Say yes.

Sara nodded. "Yes, but...you want me, too? I guess I don't understand. You want each other, so I assumed..."

Sara's voice trailed off, but Cole immediately understood what she was too shy to ask.

"We like women, too, Sara. Both of us dated women from time to time before we fell in love with each other."

Jeremy pulled her into his arms. "I can assure you we are very attracted to you. We want you, Sara. We don't go around sleeping with a bunch of different women either. You mean a great deal to us."

Sara exhaled slowly in what seemed to be relief. She smiled at both of them. "You mean a great deal to me, too. Yes, I want you. Yes, I want to be with you."

Cole tugged her down onto the bed so she was sprawled next to him. "Then come here, you gorgeous woman, and let us show you how much we want you."

He pulled her into his arms and let his hands glide over her satiny skin. His cock was ready to blow, thanks to Jeremy's foreplay, but he needed to cool down and give her some love and attention.

She was biting her lower lip again. "Um, I don't want to interrupt. You can go back to what you were doing. It was really hot watching it."

Cole hid his chuckle. Their little princess got off on watching him and Jeremy together. She really was perfect for them. He shouldn't be surprised, though. He had taken a peek at her e-reader, and it was filled with smut. The really good kind.

Jeremy grinned at Cole. "We want you to join in, honey. But we're glad that you like watching. How about giving each of us a kiss to start out with? Cole first."

Cole looked down into her green eyes, dark with passion. He lowered his head and captured her lips with his own. He ran his tongue along the seam of her mouth, and she immediately opened, welcoming his invasion. Their tongues played tag, rubbing and chasing, until both of them were groaning and breathless. Cole reluctantly lifted his head and rubbed their noses together in an Eskimo kiss.

"Jeremy's turn, honey."

* * * *

Jeremy took immediate control of the kiss. He tasted slightly minty from brushing his teeth and warm from the after-dinner scotch he enjoyed. His tongue swirled in her mouth, staking its claim and making her shake with need. Cole's hand lifted her long hair and he began to nibble along the nape of her neck, sending tingles to her already-wet pussy.

She was sandwiched between their two hard bodies, just as in her fantasies. Their fingers created magic on her touch-starved body. Her skin was on fire everywhere their hands touched and stroked. She pulled her mouth from Jeremy's, dragging in a breath. She was ready for them, and they had barely touched her.

Jeremy placed open-mouth kisses on the sensitive skin of her inner arm. Need jolted to her cunt and clit. She never knew her arms were an erogenous zone. Cole distracted her by plucking her pointed nipples through her tank top. She ground her ass against his hard cock in response. He groaned his approval. They were making her crazy. She needed them to fuck her now.

"I need you. Please fuck me!" Her voice sounded breathless and needy. It had been so long. Too damn long.

Jeremy stroked her hair back from her face. "Easy, princess. We've got all night. Jack sleeps like a rock, and Cole and I have been dreaming up ways to give you pleasure for a long time now. We've just got started."

The tidal wave that had been building inside her for weeks was overwhelming. She shook her head. "No, please don't make me wait. I need one of you inside me now. God, I need to feel something so badly."

Jeremy and Cole exchanged a look and seemed to decide in her favor. Cole tugged her tank top up and over her head, while Jeremy pulled down her sleep shorts and panties. They were so wet they tangled, but he was able to wrestle them off her legs and onto the floor. Their hungry eyes devoured her. She had never seen such lust in a man's eyes as she saw now. They looked like they wanted to eat her up.

Suddenly, Sara was a little shy. It had been more than five years since any other man had seen her naked. She crossed her arms over her small breasts. "I'm not very big up here. I hope you're not boob men."

She looked over her shoulder at her backside and giggled. "I have a little more back there. It's probably enough to hold on to."

Jeremy and Cole grinned at her sudden playfulness. Jeremy pushed her arms aside and cupped her breasts. "What can you do with more than a mouthful, princess? You've got plenty here to keep us interested."

Cole gripped her hips and pulled her ass back against his hard cock, grinding against her. Her pussy creamed in response. "This handle is fine for us. I'm an ass man, and J is a leg man. You've got great legs, too."

Sara was warm with praise. She worked out extra hard five times a week to keep her ass in the upright position and her legs trim and firm. Now she was glad she had kept up with the workouts after Jack was born. The only telltale sign she had delivered a baby was the faint silver stretch marks on her stomach.

Cole eased her down onto her back and situated himself between her legs.

"I know you said you wanted us to take you right now, but it's been a while for you, and we need to make sure you're good and wet."

Sara had never been wetter and more ready in her life. Honey coated her thighs and dripped from her pussy. She could smell her arousal in the air.

"I'm ready for you. I need you both so much."

Jeremy gave her a gentle smile. "We need you, too. But we want to give you a little pleasure first."

She almost jolted off the bed at the first touch of Cole's tongue. He swirled and nibbled at her inner thighs, making her writhe on the bed. Her blood was running hot through her veins. It made her skin feel extra sensitive.

"Hold her down, J. I can't lick her sweet pussy when she's moving around like that. I've been wanting to taste her sweet pussy for a long time."

Jeremy's strong arms held her firmly but gently still. Cole pulled one leg over his shoulder and pressed the other leg open on the mattress. She was completely exposed to his heated gaze.

Cole licked her from hole to clit. She cried out at the sensation. "Beautiful and sweet, princess. J and I are going to eat this sweet pussy every single day."

"Please, please, I can't stand it." Sara moaned her pleasure as Cole's tongue danced in her pussy and across her clit. Each lick of his tongue sent shivers through her body and brought her closer to the edge of orgasm. She trembled on the brink as Cole's tongue planted kisses as soft as butterfly wings on her pussy. She just needed a little more to go over.

Jeremy leaned down and claimed her lips, his tongue plunging into her mouth. Before she could react, Cole pressed one and then two fingers into her drenched cunt. He began to fuck her pussy in the same rhythm Jeremy fucked her mouth. Her skin was so sensitive she could have felt an eyelash brushing her. Her body was stretched taut with the maelstrom of pleasure she was experiencing. Jeremy lifted his head.

"Let her go over, Cole. She's ready."

Cole licked up to her clit, closed his mouth over the swollen bud, and sucked gently. It was exactly what she needed. Lights exploded behind her eyes as the pleasure rolled through her body. Again and again it shook her until she lay limp in Jeremy's arms. Cole lay on her other side as he held her, whispering sweet words. She opened her eyes to see both men smiling down at her.

She reached up with both hands and traced their handsome faces with her fingers.

"That was amazing. I didn't realize how much I needed to feel like someone else besides Jack's mother. Thank you."

Cole leaned in for a soft kiss. "Thank you, princess. It's a privilege that you chose us to bring you back into the land of the living."

Sara trailed her fingers down Cole's chest and explored the ridges of his muscled abs.

"I think I need to live a little more. Do you have any ideas?"

Cole grinned. "Oh yeah, J and I have some ideas, all right. You game?"

Sara laughed. She felt like she didn't have a care in the world. "Am I game? This from two men who design games? I'm game, but we have to play my games."

Jeremy quirked an eyebrow. "Your games, huh? I guess we can do that. What game did you have in mind tonight?"

"Tonight we're going to play 'Cole and Jeremy's favorite positions.'"

Cole chuckled. "I think you've been reading too many of those erotic books, princess."

Sara pouted. "And how do you know what I read? Have you been snooping?"

Cole shook his head. "No comment, but I may have overheard a few things during your book club meetings."

Sara felt her face grow warm at the thought Cole had overheard. Their reading material was not for the faint of heart. The book club liked their sex with a side of kink. Sara, especially, was drawn to the stories of dominant and submissive behavior.

Jeremy shrugged. "Nothing to be embarrassed about. We think it's hot that you enjoy reading about sex. We hope you enjoy having it even more."

She liked that they didn't judge her. "I do, especially with you two. Now who wants to show me their favorite position first?"

Cole and Jeremy laughed. "I think Cole and I would like to show you the barbecue spit. Do you know that one, princess?"

Sara certainly did. She read ménage romance like it was going out of style. She climbed onto her hands and knees. She knew one would fuck her from behind while she sucked the other off. Her pussy clenched at the erotic pictures in her mind. She was going to be fucked by something other than her vibrator.

Cole positioned himself behind Sara and Jeremy in front of her. His hard cock was inches from her face, and she licked her lips in anticipation. Jeremy smiled at her eagerness.

"Don't worry, princess. You're going to get every inch of my cock that your hot mouth can take. I can't wait to feel you suck and lick me."

Sara could see the drop of pre-cum glistening on the purplish-red mushroom head. She grasped his cock in her hand and swiped her thumb over the slit, gathering that drop and bringing it to her lips. He tasted musky and salty.

"Fuck, that's so hot. Do you like the way I taste, Sara?"

Sara nodded and ran her fingers down his velvety length. His skin was silky in contrast to the steel underneath. Jeremy groaned his approval as her hand drifted down to his heavy sac. She stroked and rolled them in her fingers, feeling the weight. She extended her tongue and lapped at his balls. His hands tangled in her long hair, tugging her mouth up.

Her mouth closed around the head of his cock, and she heard his breath come out in a hiss. She flicked her tongue on the underside before moving her lips down his steely shaft and then back up. His hands tightened in her hair as she built up speed.

"Suck him good, princess. Isn't his cock beautiful? You're going to love the taste of his cum when he fills your mouth."

Cole's dirty words enflamed her further, and she tightened her lips and flicked her tongue faster in response. She felt him push her legs farther apart, running his hands up the insides of her sticky thighs and through her drenched pussy. She moaned at the feeling of his rough hands on her cunt. She heard the crinkle of a condom wrapper.

"Fuck. Shit. When you stroked her pussy, Cole, her moans on my cock almost sent me over."

Cole lined his cock up behind her. She could feel his length brush her ass cheek before burrowing between her folds. He slowly pushed the head of his cock into her cunt, stretching the walls of her pussy wide. Slowly, inch by inch, he fed her his cock until he was finally in to the hilt. Sara exhaled slowly. Cole was big, and it had been a long time for her.

Cole stayed still and waited for her to make the first move. Sara felt the undeniable urge to move and began swaying her hips forward and then back. Tingles ran up her spine at being so firmly impaled on Cole's cock.

"Does that feel good, princess? Cole's going to fuck you so good."

Jeremy's words were prophetic. Cole began thrusting in and out of her, pulling almost all the way out and fucking her hard on the instroke. Each stroke rubbed a sweet spot inside her. She felt the inevitable climb toward release again.

Cole grabbed her hips tightly. "I'm going to ride you hard and fast, Sara. If you don't want that, say so. Otherwise, suck Jeremy's johnson and make him come."

Before Sara had a chance to giggle at the word "johnson," Cole started thrusting hard and fast, sending pleasure flowing through her body. She quickened her efforts on Jeremy's cock, shiny from her spit, and his cock seemed to swell in her mouth. He was close.

"I'm going to blow, princess. If you don't want a mouth full of cum, pull off now."

Jeremy's voice sounded strained. She couldn't wait to taste him. She laved her tongue on the sensitive underside of his cock and sucked him down until he bumped the back of her throat. He froze there for a moment before his hot cum filled her mouth. She swallowed quickly but still couldn't keep up. His cum dripped down the corner of her mouth.

Cole pulled Sara from her kneeling position so her back was against his chest. He continued thrusting into her welcoming pussy and pulled her head back to lick Jeremy's cum from her lips.

"The best of both worlds. My man's hot cum and my woman's hot pussy. It's time, Sara."

Cole reached around, rubbing circles on her already-sensitive clit. The response was immediate. Her pussy clamped down on Cole's cock, and she screamed her release as pleasure shook her from nose to toes. The pleasure seemed to go on and on, even when Cole thrust deep and held himself there. She could feel his cock jerking as he came hot and hard inside her.

They collapsed next to Jeremy on the bed, their breathing ragged.

Jeremy kissed her long and sweet before turning her to Cole for the same.

"Damn, girl. That was fucking amazing."

Sara felt truly relaxed and happy for the first time in a long time.

"I agree. You haven't said much, Jeremy."

Cole was her talker. Jeremy was her thinker.

He pulled her close and nuzzled her hair.

"I'm speechless. Words couldn't do that justice, so why try?"

Sara laughed and cuddled deeper between them. "Typical Jeremy. So practical and matter-of-fact."

Cole chuckled. "You'll get used to it and learn to love him anyway."

That was exactly what was happening. With both of them.

Chapter 7

"Welcome back. How was your vacation?"

Jeremy stood in the doorway of Steve's office. He needed to talk to his comptroller about this bank account of Scott's.

Steve grinned.

"Great. I took the family on a cruise and then did a few days at Disney. It was awesome."

Steve looked relaxed and tan. Jeremy pondered taking Cole, Sara, and Jack on a cruise. It would be a great getaway.

"I'm glad you had a great vacation. I'm afraid it's back to reality, though. I need you to look at something for me."

Steve nodded. "I already know what you're going to ask. Tina sent me an e-mail about it."

Jeremy crossed his arms and tried to look stern. "You were reading e-mails while on vacation? I ought to kick your ass, man. We're not that kind of company."

Steve just laughed at him. They had known each other since college.

"I know, I know, but I didn't want to come back to thousands of e-mails. It was no big deal. You should talk, anyway. You work constantly."

Jeremy had to admit that Steve was right. He loved what he did for a living. Creating video games was his passion. Cole's, too. But if he and Cole were going to become family men, and he hoped they would, they would need to tone down the hours at work.

Jeremy thought about how delectable Sara had looked this morning, sleepy and tousled from their lovemaking. He and Cole had tried to let her sleep in by getting Jack up, but she had insisted on making breakfast for them before they left for work. He could certainly get used to waking up with Sara between them and then her mouthwatering waffles for breakfast. They had each stolen a kiss from her on their way out the door. It had all seemed so domestic and so very…right.

Jeremy sat in the chair across from Steve. "So, if you know, what can you tell me?"

Steve shook his head. "Nothing. I don't know anything about this account except that it's for Busey Bank. I recognize the account-number pattern from our accounts there. As for why Scott would be depositing two thousand dollars a month in the account? No idea. He used a corporate credit card for travel expenses, just like you and Cole."

"What about cash expenses? Tips, cab fare, and the like?"

"He kept the receipts, and when he came into town, he would be reimbursed from petty cash."

Jeremy liked the sound of this less and less. Had Scott been involved in something unsavory? Less than legal? Jeremy remembered that Scott had loved to play poker prior to meeting and marrying Sara. He had sworn off gambling, but perhaps his addiction had led him to start again.

Steve's troubled expression mirrored his own. "I know you don't want to hear this, but I think you should call Alex on this."

Jeremy scowled. "Call a private investigator to snoop in my late brother's business? That's just fantastic. How can I do that?"

Steve leaned back and gave him a look he recognized from years of friendship. His friend was about to tell him something he didn't want to hear.

"Listen to me, Jeremy. Scott was a good guy and I'm sure a good brother. But you don't need to be the protective big brother anymore. Nothing can hurt Scott now. It will make you crazy if you don't find out about this. I know you too well."

Jeremy slumped in his chair. Steve did know him well.

"Fuck, Steve. What if I find out something horrible about Scott?"

"What if you don't?" Steve countered. "Then you can go on and know this was no big deal. End of story."

Steve picked up the receiver from the phone on his desk and handed it to Jeremy. Jeremy pulled it to his ear and punched out the familiar number of one of his best friends.

"Alex? This is Jeremy. Yeah, we need to get together for a beer real soon. How about today, in fact? I need you to look into something for me. Strictly confidential. I don't want anyone to know about this."

* * * *

Sara was vacuuming when she heard a noise at the front door. She whirled around to find a grinning Cole coming through the front door and throwing his briefcase on the foyer table.

"Hey, princess, are you hungry?"

Sara glanced at the clock and realized it was lunchtime. She had been cleaning for most of the morning.

"I could eat. What are you doing home so early?"

"I came home to take you to lunch, and then I'm going to work on this game storyboard here in the home office. I can't get a moment alone at work. Jack at playgroup?"

"Yes, with hardly a backward glance, I might add. He was having a great time and paying me absolutely no attention when I left."

Jeremy and Cole had found Jack a wonderful playgroup that would watch him a few days a week. As an only child, Sara wanted to make sure he had lots of opportunities to play with other children. He loved being with other kids and thoroughly enjoyed himself when she dropped him off for a day of playing.

"He'll be glad to see you when you pick him up. So, how about lunch? We could drive into Urbana and get lunch at the Courier Cafe."

"You had me at lunch and the Courier. I love that place, but instead of driving back into town, why don't we eat the leftover lasagna? Then we can just relax. Let me just finish vacuuming and I'll heat it up."

Cole shook his head. "Uh-uh. We told you that you didn't have to cook or clean for us. Jeremy and I have been picking up after ourselves for many years now, you know."

Sara laughed. "I know, but I like spoiling you a little. Besides, with Jack at playgroup and you and Jeremy at work, I need something to do. I've spent two weeks lounging around the house. I'm not used to this much inactivity."

"Maybe after lunch we can think of something active to do," Cole said playfully.

She wrapped her arms around Cole's lean middle and stroked his muscled back. She could feel the warmth of his body and the steady beating of his heart.

"Maybe I don't want to wait until after lunch."

Cole chuckled. "You're the princess. I'm just a lowly servant. Your wish is my command."

Sara tugged him toward the stairs.

"Actually, I was thinking we could play another game. If you're in the mood, of course."

Cole laughed. "You're the perfect woman, Sara. Jeremy and I love games, you know. What did you have in mind?"

Sara gathered her courage. So far, Cole and Jeremy seemed to be very open-minded.

"How about a game of Master and Slave? I realize Jeremy's not here, but he can play later tonight."

Cole's eyes darkened with passion. He looked like he was in favor of the game.

"Tell me what the game would entail, princess. Who's the slave, and what are the rules?"

Sara ran her hands down his arms and across his broad chest.

"You're the master and I'm the slave. The rules are simple. My body belongs to you. I have to do whatever you say. If I don't, you can punish me."

Cole gave her a look that promised sin. "Punish you? Sounds promising. I wouldn't mind turning your cute little fanny a rosy red."

Sara's pussy creamed at the thought of Cole spanking her, dominating her. This was her greatest fantasy.

"I have to disobey you first."

"Your first order, Sara. Upstairs and off with those clothes. If you aren't naked and in bed in the next ninety seconds, you'll get turned over my knee."

Sara flew up the rest of the stairs with Cole laughing behind her.

* * * *

Cole stalked up the stairs behind Sara's fleeing figure. He knew his face was covered with an evil grin. If his little princess wanted to play dominant-submissive games, he was all for it. She would soon learn she might choose the game but they would play by his and Jeremy's rules.

He pushed open the door and almost laughed out loud at the lump in the bed. Sara had pulled the covers completely over her head.

"Where's Sara? If she's not naked under those covers, she's going to get a warm bottom."

The covers shook with either laughter or fear. Cole suspected it was the former. He grasped the edge of the comforter in one hand and gave a tug. The comforter flew, and Sara lay in the middle of the bed. She was wearing her lacy bra and panties. Not naked.

So she wanted to play it that way? Game on.

"Sara, you did not follow my instructions." He gave a put-upon sigh. "You have left me no choice but to punish you."

Sara peeked at him from under her lashes. "I'm almost naked."

Cole shook his head in mock anger. "Not good enough. You're going over my knee for your disobedience. However, first things first."

Cole dropped down on the bed next to her. Her scent, soft and floral, surrounded him and swamped his senses. His cock was already hard and pressing against his zipper. He claimed her sweet lips and drank from them greedily. Her taste was so sweet and intoxicating. He let his fingers roam over her sweet curves, made to fit his hand. He loved Jeremy, but he was falling hard for Sara, too. He hoped she felt the same. He knew Jeremy did.

He lifted his head and stared down into green eyes which had turned dark with desire.

"You're going to know the penalty for disobeying me. First, undress me. But you may not touch my cock. You lost that privilege with your behavior."

Sara bit into the softness of her swollen lips. "Yes, Master."

Cole's cock tightened painfully at her honeyed tone and submissive words. Both he and Jeremy liked to be in control. If Sara was okay with that on a semi regular basis, she was never going to get rid of them.

Her hand slid up his chest and then back down, pulling the hem of his golf shirt from the waistband of his jeans. The office had a casual dress code for creative staff. Today, he was even more grateful for it. He didn't think he could stand her soft hands flicking open button after button on one of his dress shirts.

"Arms up, please, Master."

Sara kept her eyes submissively down, but he had the distinct impression she was taking the opportunity to check out the clearly outlined bulge in his jeans. Sara pulled the shirt up and off, tossing it away. She ran her hands across his chest and followed the trail of chest hair down to the button of his jeans. She popped it open before looking up at him with an expression that was pure sin.

"I'm not sure how I'm going to not touch your cock, Master. I'll try, but it's so big."

Her breathy, innocent words belied the arousal behind them. Cole could feel the lust radiating from her body. A lust that was returned tenfold.

He crossed his arms across his chest and gave her a scowl. "Flattery will get you nowhere, my little slave. I expect obedience. Failure will be punished."

"Yes, Master. I'll obey." Sara dropped her eyes again and began working the waistband down his hips and then legs. He kicked his jeans away with a devilish grin. She'd never get his boxers off without touching his cock.

Chapter 8

How am I going to get these boxers down without touching his cock?

Did she even want to obey? He'd promised a punishment, and she couldn't help but look forward to whatever he had in store for her.

She hooked her fingers in his waistband and pulled it wide, pulling it out and over his hard dick. She remembered vividly how his cock had felt in her pussy last night, and it inched her desire even higher. The crotch of her panties was soaked and her nipples tight, rubbing against the lace every time she moved, sending sparks straight to her pussy.

She pushed the boxers down his legs and tossed them into the clothing pile, feeling pretty proud of herself. She wouldn't be earning a punishment for this, but she still had one coming for not getting naked.

"Have I pleased you? What else may I do to pleasure my Lord and Master?"

Cole waved at her clothes. "Take those off. Now, my slave."

"Certainly, Master."

Sara quickly pushed her soaked panties down her legs and tossed them away. Her bra quickly followed. Cole's heated gaze touched every part of her body, making her feel desired and sexy. She could get used to feeling like this.

Cole reclined at the end of the bed. "Kneel here before me and show me how you like to be pleasured. Start with those berry-tipped breasts."

Sara could feel her skin getting red with her embarrassment. He wanted her to touch herself? In front of him?

"Are you disobeying me, my slave?"

Sara licked her suddenly dry lips. She had never had an audience before. Her perverse nature kicked in at the thought of Cole watching her. Honey dripped from her pussy down her thighs at the image she would make with her legs spread and her fingers in her cunt.

"No, Master."

She began stroking her breasts with her hands, tracing the outsides of the nipples then tickling the sensitive undersides. Her eyes closed as her fingers began twisting the hard buds, making them even tighter.

"Eyes open and on me, my slave."

Sara opened her eyes and stared into Cole's lust-filled gaze. He looked as if he was barely keeping himself in check as she stroked and kneaded her own breasts before slowly letting her hands descend toward her weeping cunt.

Cole's eyes narrowed as she knelt on the bed and spread her thighs wider. He couldn't fail to see her skin glistening with her own juices. She was incredibly turned on. Her fingers traveled between her folds, straight to her swollen clit. She circled it over and over, in her familiar rhythm, bringing her closer to orgasm. Cole's eyes never left her.

"Put your fingers inside you, my slave. Fuck yourself and pretend it's my cock."

Sara immediately obeyed, caught in the fantasy of being his slave, pleasing him completely and totally. First one finger, then a second fucked her slowly, drawing out the pleasure. She was so wet, her small fingers slipped in and out easily.

"Is that how you like to be fucked, my slave? Slowly?"

Sara's eyes wanted to close with the pleasure, but she forced them to stay open as he had commanded.

"Sometimes, Master." Her voice sounded strained to her ears. "Sometimes. But sometimes I like it hard and fast."

Cole gave her an arrogant look. "What you want is of little consequence, my slave. Your only thought should be your Master's desires."

She could feel the blood rushing to her skin, and her breathing was shallow. She was close to release.

"I'm sorry, Master. I forgot my place. It won't happen again."

Her fingers continued their slow in-and-out stroke of her pussy, glistening with her honey. "Show me how wet you are, my slave."

Sara extended her hand, and Cole leaned forward, sucking her fingers into his mouth. The sight of him sucking her hand clean almost sent her over the edge. It was erotic and naughty. Perhaps he would lick her pussy after her spanking.

He licked and sucked her fingers until they were clean before lifting his head.

"Time for your spanking, my slave. I hope this will teach you that I am in charge and you must obey. I will not tolerate your disobedience."

If Cole had expected Sara to back out, he was going to be disappointed. She was ready, and eager, for his hand to warm up her ass.

He swung his legs over the side of the bed and motioned for her to drape herself over them. She hesitated for only a second before following his instructions. Within moments, her ass was in the perfect position. He anchored his own arm around her waist. The waiting seemed like forever. She had never been spanked before but desperately wanted it.

The first smack of his hand on her ass cheeks startled her. It hurt more than she expected, and she started to protest when the sting turned to warmth. The warmth slid through her belly and straight to her pussy and clit. The second, third, and fourth smacks did more of the same. She was on the edge of orgasm and desperately needed to come.

She lost count as the spanking heated not only her ass but her entire cunt. She was dripping cream when he ended the spanking, stroking her sore ass cheeks with gentle fingers.

"Will you disobey me again, my slave?"

"No, Master. Please, please, let me come!" Sara wriggled on his lap, trying to get his fingers where she wanted them. She was rewarded with a sharp slap to her already-sore bottom.

"Stop it, my slave. I decide when you get your pleasure."

She almost sagged on his lap, defeated, before he added, "You took your punishment well. You deserve a reward."

Then his fingers were exactly where she needed them. It took mere seconds of stimulating her clit before she cried out with relief. She came hard, harder than she ever had. The pleasure was so intense she shook from it. His talented fingers drew out the waves until she lay over his lap, wrung out and spent.

* * * *

Cole's cock was painfully hard, and his balls were pulled up and tight. Spanking Sara's creamy, heart-shaped ass had him practically coming all over himself. Add in her delightful response to being dominated and Cole was in heaven with this woman.

He carefully lifted her and set her on his lap, holding her gently until awareness came over her. She lifted her eyes to his, holding his gaze for long moments before caressing his jaw with her soft hand.

"That was amazing."

Cole felt his throat constrict with the force of his feelings. "Yeah, amazing. I like your game."

Sara smiled, tracing his lips with her fingers. His mouth tingled from the contact as if she had kissed him.

"Hmmm…I love the game, too. I think this is going to be one of my favorites. But we're not done, are we…Master?"

Sara wiggled on his dick. He was hard as concrete, and her movements sent arrows of pleasure straight to his balls and up his spine. He didn't want to come. Yet.

"No, we are not done, my slave. Lie down on the bed and spread your legs. Wide. I want to see the pussy that belongs to me. If you're a good, obedient slave, you may get to come again."

Cole chuckled to himself as Sara scrambled to get into position. Her legs were spread wide, and he could see her thighs were sticky from her arousal. The dark curls between her legs were damp and her pretty, pink pussy peeked out at him, beckoning.

He leaned over her, taking in her gorgeous body. She was tiny but with enough curves to satisfy both he and Jeremy. Her skin glowed with the sunlight streaming into the room. The rays caressed each slope and plane of her luscious form.

He extended his tongue and laved at her nipples. They'd gone soft after her climax. He would get them hard again. He sucked one in, scraping his tongue across the edges. Sara moaned, and her eyes fluttered closed. He repeated the motion until both nipples were hard and tight and Sara was writhing underneath him. She looked beautiful—her long, dark hair spread over the pillow, her skin flushed with arousal, her breath coming in pants. She was ready for him.

He pulled open the nightstand drawer and grabbed a condom. At once, a vision of Sara holding a blond baby flashed before his eyes. He wondered if she wanted more children. She was a wonderful mother. They would talk about it soon, he hoped.

He rolled on the condom and positioned his cock at the opening of her pussy.

"Do you want my cock, my slave? Do you want me to fuck you?"

Sara nodded vigorously, wrapping her arms around his shoulders.

"Yes, please, Master. Please fuck me."

Cole slowly, torturously, pushed his cock into her tight, wet cunt. Fighting the urge to thrust hard and to the hilt, he forced himself to enter her in a controlled fashion, her pussy stretching to accommodate him. He hoped she wasn't sore from the hard fucking he had given her last night. Luckily, her expression was one of pleasure, not pain, as he continued his relentless pressure until he was all the way in and his balls slapped her ass cheeks.

He closed his eyes and took deep breaths to hold back his release. Her pussy hugged him like a hot velvet glove. He never wanted to leave it. He pulled out slowly and pushed back in slowly. Over and over, slowly, driving them both mad with want and need, he fucked her. Never increasing the speed, even when she threw her legs around his hips and bucked against him. She dug her nails into his shoulders, urging him to go faster, harder, anything to make her come.

"I thought this is how you liked it, my slave. You touched yourself slowly, so I'm fucking you slowly."

Sara shook her head back and forth on the pillow. "No, Master! Fuck me hard! I need it!"

Cole couldn't ignore the plea in her voice and the building pressure in his balls.

"Whatever my princess wants, she gets."

Cole increased the speed of his thrusts, slamming into her pussy hard and fast. She mewled in pleasure each time his groin rubbed against her clit. The rippling of her pussy told him she was close. He reached in between them to rub circles around her clit.

Her pussy clamped down on his cock as she fell apart in his arms. She screamed his name as the force of her orgasm shook her slight body. He thrust in to the hilt one last time, feeling his cock jerk and spasm as he filled the condom with his seed. The pleasure burst from his balls, through his cock, and up his spine. Mary and Joseph, it was so good.

He collapsed on top of her, their bodies slick with sweat and her honey.

"I swear I'll get off of you in a minute. I know I'm crushing you."

He felt rather than heard Sara's giggle then her push on his shoulder. He rolled off of her.

"You are pretty heavy. But you're worth it."

He grabbed some tissues from the nightstand and quickly took care of the condom. He pulled her close and cuddled her soft form. He felt a tightening in his heart at the thought they might not be able to persuade her to stay. She had become incredibly important to him, to them, in such a short time. They wanted her and Jack to stay.

He traced a pattern on her soft skin. She shivered in response. He loved that she was so responsive.

"I think we missed lunch, princess."

Sara yawned and cuddled closer. "I'm not hungry now, actually. I'd rather cuddle with you. How about telling me a story?"

"A story, huh? What kind of story?" Sara often made up silly stories for Jack.

"How about the story of how you and Jeremy got together? I've never heard that one."

Cole smiled at the memory. "I remember it like it was yesterday. The day I met Jeremy was the day I showed up for a job interview at the company. I saw Jeremy and fell immediately in lust."

Sara frowned. "Not in love?"

Cole chuckled at her expression. "Not at first. But I thought he was handsome, sexy, and dynamic. He was also about to become my boss. I actually tried to throw the interview so he wouldn't hire me and I could ask him out. It didn't work obviously. He hired me anyway. That started my work crush on him. Man, I loved going to work every day just to see him, spend time with him."

"How did you two get together then if he was your boss? That's sexual harassment, you know."

"That I well know, and so did Jeremy. He told me later he found me attractive, too, but of course didn't do anything because of our employer-employee status. Finally, I couldn't take it anymore. I wasn't eating or sleeping for thinking about him. I didn't care about the job. I walked into Jeremy's office and slapped my resignation on his desk."

Sara sat straight up. "What happened?"

"He offered me more money. I was crazed, Sara. I couldn't take it anymore. I told him that I didn't want more money, I wanted him."

Sara's eyes were round with amazement. "Um, how did he take that?"

Cole grinned. "We had sex on his desk. Been together ever since."

Sara laughed. "On his desk, huh?"

"Yep, we've moved to a bigger building, but he's never gotten rid of that desk. I get hard just walking into his office thinking about that morning. Hmmm...we'll have to christen that desk again—only with you this time."

Sara turned a becoming shade of pink. "In the office? What if someone heard? Oh my God, did anyone hear you?"

Cole shrugged. "It was early in the morning, so I doubt it. But at the time I didn't give a tinker's damn. I was out of the closet by then, and Jeremy was, too. That was eleven years ago. I've grown up a lot since then. I probably wouldn't handle it quite the same, but I would make damn sure the outcome was still the same."

Sara nibbled at her swollen lower lip, stirring his cock again. "This closet thing? You said you dated women, too. Have you dated since being with Jeremy?"

"I wouldn't call it dating. We've had some evenings with women who wanted a fling with two men. We wanted to be with a woman. I love Jeremy and want to spend my life with him, but we like having a woman between us. Specifically, we like having you between us."

Sara yawned, wider this time. "I like being between you. Not sure how I feel about those other women, though."

Cole pulled her closer, his hand tangling in her silky hair. "Sleep, my princess. They didn't mean anything. It was all fun and games, and everyone knew the score. This is something different."

Cole lay there, feeling her warm body and listening to her even breathing as she slept. His heart was lost to this tiny woman. He and Jeremy had to find a way to make her stay.

Chapter 9

"Did you talk to Steve today?" Cole speared the last piece of chicken with his fork and popped it in his mouth. Sara had made chicken piccata and a salad for dinner, and Cole had been starving. He and Sara had worked up quite an appetite playing Master and Slave this afternoon.

Jeremy studied his chicken closely. "I have someone looking into it."

"I would have thought Steve would have known about it right away."

"He had a lot of things going on today. It's his first day back from a two-week vacation."

Jeremy's voice had taken on a sharper edge than normal. Cole gave him a look, but Jeremy avoided his eyes. Luckily, Sara was so busy trying to get a recalcitrant Jack to eat she didn't notice the byplay.

"C'mon, Jack, one more bite? For Mommy? It's okay, Cole. Jeremy will get to the bottom of it." Sara gave Jeremy a dazzling smile.

"I certainly will," Jeremy agreed.

Sara scooped Jack up in her arms and headed for the stairs. "I think he's more tired than hungry. I'm going to start his bath and get him to bed."

"Cole and I will take care of cleaning up, and then we'll be up to read him a story."

Once Sara was safely out of earshot, Cole turned to Jeremy. "Okay, what's up? Steve should have taken one look at that account number and known what it was. He has an amazing memory for numbers."

Jeremy nodded grimly. "Steve's never seen the account and doesn't know what it's for. I called in Alex."

Cole was glad he was sitting down. "You called in a private investigator? What the fuck for?"

Jeremy rested his forehead in his hands for a moment. "What if Scott was involved in something he shouldn't have been? You know he liked to play poker before he married Sara. I'm concerned about this secret account. I also gave Alex the e-mail address Sara gave us where the statements were mailed. He'll get to the bottom of it. Hopefully, it's nothing. But I need to know why my late brother had secrets from his wife."

Cole leaned back in his chair. "Are we sure we want to know? What do we gain from finding this out?"

Jeremy pushed back his chair and started pacing the kitchen. "What if Scott owed people money? I don't want them to come after Sara and Jack. I can't risk their safety."

"Fuck, J. Sweet Mary, I never thought about that. I'm glad we have Sara and Jack here with us. We can keep an eye out for them."

Jeremy nodded in agreement. "We just need to find out the truth. What was Scott doing in the final months of his life?"

* * * *

The wrist shackles held her in place firmly and at his mercy. The leg spreader held her legs open and her pussy vulnerable. She should have been frightened but instead was aroused. He circled her, studying her. His gaze raked over her body, held prisoner for his pleasure. He looked at her so intently she could feel the heat from his gaze. She could hide nothing from him.

"Who does this belong to?" His hand swept from head to toe, his face a scowl.

"You."

"You, what?" He scowled further.

"You, Sir!" Her voice was thick with desire. Desire to be owned by him.

"That's better, little sub." He continued his perusal, making her squirm. Why didn't he touch her?

"You are undisciplined. You must learn to obey me in all things and give your body over to me. Are you ready to do that, little sub?"

"Yes, Sir. Very much, Sir." She tugged at the restraints futilely. She didn't want to get free, but he was so handsome, her fingers itched to touch him.

He stood before her so tall and handsome. His shoulders broad and his abs a perfect six-pack. He had left his jeans on but taken off everything else. Her eyes were drawn to the large bulge in his pants.

"Stop that. You'll bruise my property. From now on, you will care for your body respectfully, as it no longer belongs to you. You will eat nutritious food, exercise regularly, and drink no alcohol. Any pleasure this body receives will come from me and me alone. I, alone, will decide if you receive any pleasure. Your pleading and begging will have no effect on me."

She licked her dry lips. She wanted to belong to him and only him.

"I live to serve you, Sir. Your pleasure is my only desire."

He nodded his head briefly. "So be it. The life you knew is no more. Your new life, as my love and my submissive, starts now."

"Whew! This is one hot BDSM book." Tori's face was pink.

Sara couldn't help but agree. The book was sensual and arousing without being overdone. "Yeah, very hot. This Dom is sexy. I can picture him in those jeans. They'd be tight and showing off his very bitable ass. Yowza!"

Brianne groaned. Her stomach was huge and her feet were propped up to keep her ankles from swelling. She looked ready to pop any minute.

"Stop it. I've been too huge to have any fun with Nate for a month. I'm huge and horny. I don't know why I'm even reading this stuff. I must be a masochist."

Noelle laughed. "You and Nate aren't doing the dirty deed? It must indeed be a cold day in hell. You guys were my sexual heroes."

Brianne scowled. Sara knew the Florida heat and humidity hadn't put her in the best of moods. "It's not for lack of trying on my part, believe me. Nate loves my pregnant belly and thinks I'm sexy as hell, but the way this baby is sitting, sex is uncomfortable. Not to mention every time I, you know, I feel like I'm going to go into labor."

Tori's brows knitted. "You know? You mean, have an orgasm? I don't remember feeling that way."

Lisa laughed. "Just goes to show you how strong her 'you knows' are with Nate."

Tori laughed, too. "Good point. I don't remember strong 'you knows' when I was pregnant."

Lisa threw her e-reader on the side table. "So, Sara, when are you coming home?"

"We're throwing a birthday party slash Fourth of July barbecue this weekend for Jack. I don't really know when we're coming back. Cole and Jeremy want me to stay the rest of the summer."

Sara wasn't sure if she ever wanted to leave. Cole and Jeremy liked to play sex games as much as she did. They were completely open-minded and nonjudgmental. There were still so many games they hadn't played yet.

Noelle sipped at her flirtini. "We miss you, but at least we get to see you once a week thanks to Skype. But you won't be here when Brianne has the baby. I doubt she'll last more than a few days more."

"Hey! I'm sitting right here. And God, I hope you're right. I feel like a beached whale. I can't eat, I can't sleep. I can't even have a cosmo to help myself sleep. I'm trying to convince Nate to take me to Busch Gardens to ride the roller coasters. I hear that will bring on labor."

Tori shuddered. "And probably projectile vomiting, in your condition. I heard you should watch the movie *Raging Bull*."

Lisa nodded. "I heard that, too."

Noelle waved them off. "I heard that you should eat spicy food. That's what my mom says anyway. She ate some habanero peppers and went into labor with my little sister."

Brianne sighed. "Can we change the subject? I'm getting a little nauseous at the idea of eating spicy food. Sara, did you find out anything about the bank account Scott had?"

Sara shook her head. "No, but Jeremy has someone looking into it. He'll find out what it was for."

"Sara," Tori said carefully, "how difficult is it to find out if it's one of their accounts? I don't mean to be tough on Jeremy, but this doesn't seem like the mystery of the century. Is it one of their accounts or not?"

"It's not that it's difficult. It's that the guy who would know just got back from a big vacation and he's slammed trying to catch up. He'll get to it. I didn't know about it for fifteen months, so a few days more isn't going to make any difference. Besides, I'm sure it's just some sort of business account. We never had any financial problems, so the money couldn't have been ours to begin with. It must belong to the business somehow. You know how Scott was, he was always thinking about business. That was really his first love."

* * * *

Jeremy carefully placed the hamburgers on the hot grill. It was a sunny and hot Fourth of July, and the backyard was full of guests. Sara was flitting around with Jack on her hip filling cold drinks and making party small talk. She looked beautiful today in a red-flowered sundress and her hair pulled back with a matching red hair tie. Jack was charming the guests and lapping up the attention. He spied Steve out of the corner of his eye making his way to the grill.

"Hey, boss. Why don't you let me watch the grill? Alex is in your study. I think he has the information you've been waiting for."

Jeremy was silent for a moment. He hated that he had to call in Alex and wondered for a moment if he shouldn't just let things be. But he knew that he couldn't go on wondering. The last few days, although heaven with Sara, had been difficult.

Jeremy didn't want to lie to Sara. Luckily, she hadn't asked him again about the bank account. In a way, it only made him feel even worse. The reason she hadn't asked was she trusted him to take care of it.

Things had been so amazing between the three of them. Jeremy and Cole had been delighted to learn that Sara was sexually adventurous. She was playful, sweet, sexy, and creative. After he had found out she had played Master and Slave with Cole, he had made her promise to play a game of Pirate and Captive Slave with him. She had readily agreed and even thrown in a few more game ideas of her own.

"Did he tell you what he found?"

Steve shook his head. "Nope. None of my damn business. If you need me to do anything, just let me know. But otherwise, I'm on a need-to-know basis."

Jeremy felt relieved. Steve was like family, but this was pretty personal.

"Thanks, man. I'll head back there now."

Jeremy glanced over at Sara talking to the neighbors. If he hurried she'd never miss him.

* * * *

Jeremy snagged Cole's arm and pulled him toward the office. "What? Where are we going, J? Are you in the mood now?"

Cole playfully grabbed at Jeremy's ass but froze when he saw the look on his face.

"What's going on, J?"

Jeremy pulled him into the office, and Cole didn't need to wonder what was going on anymore. Alex was sitting in a chair, holding a folder.

He tugged Jeremy down onto the love seat with him. If it was bad news, it was best to take it sitting down.

Alex set the folder down on the coffee table between them and flipped it open, scattering photos. Cole couldn't resist the urge to pick one up. It was a picture of a pretty teenage girl. Cole wasn't good at guessing ages but she was maybe sixteen or seventeen.

"I'm not sure where to begin, but I guess I'll start with the bank account. Your brother, Scott, had been paying two thousand dollars a month for four years before his death to a bank account in Champaign. That account belongs to Carrie Stewart. Does that name ring a bell, Jeremy?"

Jeremy shook his head. "No, should it?"

"Not necessarily. You might have some memory of her. She was Scott's high school girlfriend his senior year."

"I was already at college by then. Scott had a lot of girlfriends over the years until Sara. Why was Scott giving her money, for God's sake?"

Cole could feel the tension in Jeremy's body. He rubbed Jeremy's hand with his own, trying to calm him down.

Alex sighed and held up the picture of the teenage girl. "This is Stacey Parker. She's eighteen years old and heading to the University of Illinois in the fall. A pretty girl, isn't she? She's Carrie's daughter."

Alex pushed the photo in front of Jeremy. "And she's Scott's daughter. If you look, you can see the resemblance."

Jeremy's eyes widened in astonishment. "His daughter? Scott had a daughter and never told anyone? I can't believe that. Scott couldn't even keep Christmas presents a secret for a few days. He was the worst liar in the world. There's no way he could keep this a secret. You've made a mistake, Alex."

"I wish I had, Jeremy. I talked to Ms. Stewart, now Parker, myself once I knew the basics. It seems she got pregnant before graduation but didn't realize it until afterward. By then, Scott had gone off for the summer to Europe, and her parents shipped her off to a relative to have the baby. She intended to put the baby up for adoption but at the last minute changed her mind. At that point, she didn't want to tell Scott. She just wanted to move forward. She met a young man, and they married shortly after. He raised Stacey as his own until the couple divorced about ten years ago."

Alex picked up a few more photos and placed them in front of Jeremy. "Ms. Stewart never intended to tell Scott about Stacey. But Scott was visiting town about five years ago when he ran into Ms. Stewart and her daughter in a store. He instantly recognized his old girlfriend, noticed her daughter looked so much like him, did the math, and well, Scott was never stupid. He realized Stacey was his daughter.

"According to Ms. Stewart, she knew that Scott was married and madly in love with his wife. She didn't want to be any trouble between them. She said she respected that Scott had other commitments. Scott insisted on helping financially. After all, she was a single parent and she could use the help. As time went by, Scott would come by more often to spend time with Stacey. She said he was a good father and Stacey grew to love him very much. They were devastated when they heard he had passed away. They both came to the services, they said."

Cole shook his head in amazement. "Half the town was at the services. We were so shocked by Scott's death I don't think I could tell you who was there. It's a blur."

Jeremy's jaw was tight. "That explains why Sara was saying that Scott spent so much time traveling for work. I was always puzzled by that. When she got pregnant, we arranged that Scott wouldn't travel more than one week a month. But he was coming up here, wasn't he?"

Alex nodded. "From the records I was able to find, he spent two weeks a month in Florida and two weeks here in Champaign with his daughter."

Cole felt his anger rising, and he jumped up to pace the room. "And did he pick up where he left off with his old girlfriend? Was he unfaithful to Sara?"

Alex held up his hand. "Now wait a minute. From what I can tell the answer is an unequivocal no. Ms. Stewart said that it was very clear that Scott was in love with his wife. Neither of them had any feelings left for one another. I believed her as she hadn't been all that starry-eyed over him as a teenager, either. She never wanted to tie herself to him by having his baby."

"What about the money? Didn't she wonder where the money was coming from even after Scott died?" Cole sat back down heavily. This was almost too much to take in. Jeremy's brother had been living a secret life.

"She said she thought that Jeremy had set it up like some sort of trust fund that would go on even after his death. When she found out that Sara had funded the account last month, she tried to give me a check for the money. She said she never wanted to take anything from Sara."

Alex leaned forward. "I didn't take the check. They're not destitute, but believe me, two thousand dollars is probably a lot of money to her."

It was Jeremy's turn to stand up and pace. "I need to think about this, Alex. I don't want to leave them with nothing. It sounds like they've been counting on that money every month. This is Scott's daughter. My niece, for fuck's sake."

Alex stood, leaving the file on the table. "I know you'll do the right thing, my friend. I'll leave all of this with you, and you can look through the evidence. I need to get back home now. My daughter is none too happy about my working today."

Jeremy gave Alex a strained smile. "I really appreciate this, man. Can't you stay for the party? It's Jack's birthday."

Alex shook his head and headed for the door. "I wish I could, but Kaley has plans for us today. Happy Fourth, guys. Call me and we'll have a couple of beers."

Cole moved forward to usher Alex out but was waved off. "I know my way out. I've been here a couple hundred times. You two have a lot to talk about."

Jeremy and Cole just sat silently for a while after Alex left. Cole didn't even know what to say to his lover. He pulled Jeremy close, holding him for long moments.

Finally Cole lifted his head and looked into Jeremy's eyes. "We have to tell her, J."

Jeremy's expression was pale and grim. "How do we do that, babe? Oh hey, Sara, the husband you adored and had a son with? Well, he was a big fat liar living a secret life. Fuck, that should go over great."

"I don't know exactly how we're going to tell her, but we have to tell her. She has a right to know."

Jeremy wiped his hand down his face. "I know we do, and we will. But, shit, not today. Let's try to absorb what happened today and figure out a good time to tell her. I'm not afraid to say that I'm afraid of her reaction. What if she thinks we're only trying to ruin Scott's memory so she'll move on and fall in love with us? Or worse, what if she thinks we really knew all this time and covered up for Scott? This is going to hurt Sara terribly. I don't see any way that she comes out of this unscathed."

"You're right. Sara is going to be hurt. But she's a strong woman, J. Your big brother instincts are kicking in, I can tell. You don't need to protect Scott's memory, and you don't need to protect Sara. You can't fix everything, J. Even you aren't that powerful."

Jeremy gave him a wry smile. "I sure don't feel powerful at the moment. I feel helpless. We're going to have to hurt the woman we love. You do love her, don't you?"

Cole pulled him close again. "Fuck yeah. And we're all going to live happily ever after. Believe it, J. I can feel it in my bones. I'm not wrong about this."

Chapter 10

Sara hit the "Start" button on the dishwasher and leaned against the kitchen counter with a sigh. It had been a wonderful party. Jeremy and Cole's friends had welcomed her and Jack with open arms. It appeared that more than a few friends assumed that she, Jeremy, and Cole were involved. She was surprised to find that no one had any issues with it. Little did they know she would be back in Florida, leading her solitary life before too long. Her time with Jeremy and Cole wouldn't last forever.

Jack had received more toys than any two-year-old should ever have. Jeremy and Cole had given him a police car he could sit in and pedal around Flintstone-style. Jack had been in heaven and had pressed the siren button most of the afternoon and then laughed with delight. They had also given him blocks, a Green Lantern action figure, and a set of educational DVDs. Cole had said he couldn't find any educational video games he liked and that he needed to design one. Apparently, Jack had inspired a new line of products for the company.

She felt a hand slide around her waist and pull her back against his hard body. She breathed deeply and let her lungs fill with his scent. Woodsy. Jeremy. She pressed back against him, feeling his cock harden against her bottom. These men were always ready, and she loved it.

"You look very pensive, princess. Worn out from the party?" Jeremy's voice tickled her ear.

She shook her head. "Not really. Just run down from all the excitement. Jack was worn out, too. He fell asleep immediately after his bath."

Thank goodness, he had also slept through the sounds of the fireworks. He was a good sleeper.

She felt Jeremy's chuckle. "He had a big day. I thought he might be hyper after eating the birthday cake, but he was fine."

Sara elbowed Jeremy in the ribs. "No thanks to you and Cole. You spoil him. I think he wanted to sleep in his police car. How am I ever going to get that home, anyway?"

"Let's worry about that when the time comes. Are you ready for bed, my angel?" Jeremy's lips nuzzled the crook of her neck, sending sparks of arousal coursing through her veins.

"Mmmmm...definitely. I've been thinking of a new game."

Jeremy nipped her earlobe and soothed it with his tongue. "Name the game, princess."

Sara tilted her head to give him better access and was rewarded with nibbling kisses across her bare shoulders. Her pussy creamed in anticipation of the pleasure he and Cole could bring her.

"Mistress and slaves."

Jeremy lifted his head and turned her around. He looked like he was trying hard not to laugh.

"*Mistress* and slaves? Just who are these slaves?"

Sara gave him a playful smile. "Why, you and Cole, of course."

Jeremy gave her an arrogant look. "I'm not so sure about this game."

Cole swung into the kitchen with a trash bag stuffed full. "Did I hear 'game?' What are we playing tonight?"

Jeremy rolled his eyes. "Mistress and slaves. Guess who the slaves are?"

Cole grinned as he tied off the trash bag and placed it on the other side of the garage door. Tomorrow was trash day.

"I'll go out on a limb and guess that you and I are the slaves, J. Sounds like fun. I'm in."

Jeremy playfully scowled.

"I haven't gotten to be the Master yet."

Sara smacked his arm. "You got to be Pirate Captain just the other night. That's pretty close."

Jeremy sighed. "Okay, you're the Mistress and we're the slaves. But just this once. I like to be in charge."

Sara giggled. "Just this once. Now shuck those clothes and head to the bedroom. I want you both naked and on your knees."

The men looked at each other in surprise.

Sara crossed her arms across her chest and gave them her best stern look. "Now, slaves. I know where the paddles are kept in this house. Move!"

Cole grinned and headed quickly upstairs, tugging on his clothes all the way up. Jeremy followed more slowly. Seemed like she had a reluctant slave on her hands.

* * * *

Cole couldn't hold back his smile as he and Jeremy waited on their knees in the bedroom. They were both naked as the day they were born, and despite Jeremy's grouchiness about the game, they both sported enormous erections. Cole had to hold himself back from reaching out to stroke Jeremy's cock.

Sara entered the bedroom. One look at her and Cole almost had a stroke. Sara was dressed in a skintight, black micromini skirt and a black corset laced up the front. Her shapely legs were encased in fishnet, thigh-high stockings and bright-red fuck-me heels. Her long dark hair was pulled up in a long ponytail. The outfit was completed by the riding crop she held in one hand and tapped against her stocking-clad thigh. She looked like a male submissive's wet dream.

Cole wasn't submissive by nature, but at this moment he could see the appeal.

"I see my slaves followed my command."

Sara circled them, trailing the end of the crop across their shoulders and down their chests. She stood in front of them with a stern expression. She used the tip of the crop to tap on the inside of their thighs.

"Spread your knees wider, boys. I want to see what you have for your Mistress."

Cole pushed his knees wider as did Jeremy. Jeremy was even more dominant than Cole. He wasn't sure how Jeremy was taking this. One glance at Jeremy's cock assuaged any fears. It was purple-red, and pre-cum had already started leaking from the tip. Jeremy was as turned on as he was.

"Very impressive. Your cocks are beautiful and please me very much. But before I let you fuck me, there are a few things you need to do first."

Shit, I need to fuck her now.

"Face each other."

Cole and Jeremy turned to face each other. Cole could smell Jeremy's distinct woodsy scent. It was one of the first things he had noticed about Jeremy that first day in the office. It could still get him hard and horny all these years later.

"Hands behind your back. Now kiss each other. Like you fucking mean it."

They needed no second prompting. Their lips met and tongues tangled as they fought for control of the kiss. It seemed to go on forever before they came up for air. They were breathing hard as they pulled back, staring deep into each other's eyes. Jeremy's eyes were dark blue with passion.

"I enjoyed watching that, my slaves. You may kiss again and use your hands on each other. But don't touch your cocks. Yet."

Sara's voice was husky. She was getting turned on watching them. She really was the perfect woman.

They kissed again, more slowly this time, tongues sliding and rubbing, while hands caressed and stroked. Cole ran his hand down Jeremy's muscular back, the muscles bunching under his fingers. The skin was so smooth in comparison. Their cocks were trapped between their bodies, and they rubbed together a little. Jeremy's pre-cum smeared on Cole's belly.

"Stop."

Cole pulled from Jeremy's arms reluctantly. He was on the edge and needed to come badly, but he trusted Sara to take care of them.

Sara pulled a chair from the corner of the room to a spot in front of them. She would have a ringside seat to anything she asked them to do. She hooked a leg over each arm of the chair, and her skirt tucked up almost to her waist. The position exposed her pretty pink pussy to their gazes. She was wet and swollen. Cole licked his lips in anticipation of licking her sweet cream. He smiled as he saw Jeremy do the same.

Sara reached down between her legs and began to stroke her pussy and clit. She sighed as her fingers swirled in her juices.

"Hmmm…that feels good. Do you want some pussy, boys?"

* * * *

Cole's and Jeremy's eyes were hungry as they stared at her exposed cunt. Their cocks were hard and their balls drawn up. She needed to let them come soon. These last few weeks the three of them had explored their sexuality in ways she had only dreamed of. This was the next step. She wanted to watch them together. They had been careful not to be together in front of her for some reason. She had heard them in the shower, and it had made her wet just listening. Tonight she would watch.

"You have to earn my pussy. Jeremy, suck Cole's cock. I want to see him come in your mouth."

Jeremy flashed her a smile. "May we change positions, Mistress?"

Sara waved her hand. "You may move about in any way."

Jeremy pushed Cole up to sit on the bed with Jeremy on his knees. She shivered as Jeremy's hands ran up Cole's legs, pressing his thighs apart to insinuate himself in between. She remembered those hands on her body. They were pure magic.

Jeremy leaned over and began licking Cole up and down, getting his cock shiny with saliva, before sucking the head into his mouth. Cole's eyes closed in ecstasy as his partner began moving his head up and down. Sara could hear the wet, sucking sounds, and her own pussy responded by gushing more cream on her fingers. She wanted to come but ruthlessly pushed the thought away. This was about Cole and Jeremy.

Jeremy's fingers rolled Cole's sac, and he grabbed the top of Jeremy's head.

"I'm coming, baby. I'm going to shoot my load."

Cole's voice was hoarse, but Jeremy heard him and doubled his efforts. Cole shoved his cock into Jeremy's mouth one last time with a groan. Jeremy's throat worked to swallow the cum that filled his mouth. Sara couldn't peel her eyes away. This was the hottest porn she had ever watched.

Jeremy licked Cole clean before sitting back on his knees. He gave her an evil grin.

"Did I please you, Mistress?"

It took a moment for Sara to find her voice. "Yes, you did. And Cole, too, from the look of things. Now, I want you to fuck Cole. Any position, but make sure you give it to him good. I want you to be as satisfied as you made him. Cole is not to come again, though. I'll be using his cock soon."

"Assume the position, baby." Jeremy gave Cole a smirk. Cole must have known what Jeremy meant, because he laughed and turned so that he was kneeling on the bed, his ass in the air. His backside was at the perfect level for a good hard fucking from behind. Sara moved from her chair to sit at the head of the bed. She reached into the nightstand for the bottle of lube she knew lived there and tossed it to him.

Jeremy caressed Cole's backside and leaned over to trail kisses down his back. Sara was touched at the show of tenderness and love. What would it be like to be loved by these two wonderful men? She shook the thought away. They loved each other. There wouldn't be room in their hearts for her, too, no matter how much they tried to convince her to stay. She shouldn't wish for things that she could never have. She had certainly learned that these last months. It was better to deal in what she could have. At least for tonight, she could have these men.

"Fuck him good, Jeremy. Then he's going to fuck me."

* * * *

Jeremy's dick was so hard it ached. He needed to be balls deep in Cole. Now. He lined up his cock with Cole's back hole and pushed forward, groaning as Cole's tight ass surrounded him. Jeremy knew he wouldn't last long. Between Cole's stranglehold on his dick and Sara watching them with lust-filled eyes he was on the edge already.

He pulled out and slammed back in. Cole groaned, pushing back. After all these years, Jeremy knew that Cole liked it hard and dirty. He wouldn't disappoint him. He leaned over and locked eyes with Sara while he whispered in Cole's ear.

"Can you feel my cock in your ass, baby?" He pulled out and slammed back in. "Can you feel it? How does it feel to have my dick pounding your ass? Tell me or I won't fuck you."

Cole pushed back against him. "Damn you, Jeremy. Fuck me, you asshole."

Jeremy moved his cock back and forth in small motions very slowly. He was running his dick over Cole's prostate and probably driving him crazy. Sara's eyes were wide as she watched him fuck Cole ever so slowly. Was she imagining him in her ass? He vowed that tonight she was going to feel him there.

"How does my cock feel, baby? Do you love it? Tell me and I'll fuck you hard."

Cole loved the dirty talk, Jeremy knew.

Cole panted. "Yes, I love it. I love your big cock, you fucking asshole. Now fuck me with it."

Jeremy needed no further prodding. He rode Cole's ass fast and hard. They were both breathing heavy and groaning. Sara's eyes never moved from his as his sac drew up and the pressure in his balls became unbearable. He thrust in one last time and held himself there as his orgasm racked his body. He shot his seed deep into Cole's ass, marking his man as he had done so many times before. This time was different, special. Sara was with them now.

He pulled from Cole's warmth and slumped on the mattress, pulling him close. Cole loved the raunchiness of the act. Jeremy loved it, too, but cherished the closeness afterward. He stroked his hands over Cole's sweaty body, loving the feel of the hard muscles under his fingers. Cole's cock was standing up proud and erect again. Hopefully, Sara had plans for his lover. Jeremy certainly had plans for her. It was time the tables were turned on their little Mistress. He levered himself from the bed and whispered quickly in Cole's ear.

Chapter 11

Sara had never been more turned on in her life. Watching Jeremy and Cole make love had been amazing. She snuggled in with them on the bed, closing her eyes against her own raging need. This was about them tonight. She wanted to be as unselfish as they had been to her. Sara's arm draped over Cole, and her fingers stroked over Jeremy's. He quickly entangled them together. Jeremy was quiet, but he was also her snuggler. He loved being close and would hold her all night. Tonight they held Cole between them, feeling the warmth of his skin.

She felt the bed move but kept her eyes closed. She could hear water running in the bathroom. Jeremy must be cleaning up.

Cole moved slightly away to run his hands up and down her bare arms.

"This outfit is really something, princess. It's going to look even better in a heap on the floor."

Before Sara could react to Cole's cornball line, she felt strong arms tugging her arms behind her back. Whisper-smooth silk ran over her skin, binding her wrists together at the small of her back. It had probably taken only moments. She tugged at the restraints, her eyes wide open now and taking in two smiling men.

"What are you two doing? I'm in charge tonight." She tugged a little harder on the ties but didn't succeed in budging them at all. She had always fantasized about being tied up and helpless. Her body was reacting to the situation by dripping cream down her thighs and tightening her nipples. *Damn.*

Jeremy crossed his arms over his chest, highlighting his muscled arms. He gave her a wicked grin. "Well, the thing about that is, you're not anymore. Cole and I are your Masters now, and from now on, I might add. Not that your little foray into Mistress land wasn't fun. It was. But things need to return to their natural order. And the natural order in this house doesn't include me on my knees. Stand up, little slave."

For a moment, Sara thought about resisting but quickly pushed the thought from her head. This was exactly what she wanted, and they all knew it. She pushed to her knees on the bed and then scooted back to step on the floor, teetering for just a second on her high heels.

"I don't want you hurting yourself. Cole, help me take these shoes off of her."

Jeremy knelt down with Cole on the other side, quickly stripping her of her shoes and the thigh-high stockings while they were at it.

"I'm a leg man, honey, and you looked really hot in that outfit, but when I fuck you tonight, I don't want anything between me and your soft skin." Jeremy ran his finger across her cleavage.

Cole came up behind her and began tugging at the tie that held her hair. "Where'd you get the outfit anyway? I don't think Champaign-Urbana has a BDSM store, but I could be wrong."

"Online. I had it shipped two-day. You didn't notice it with the presents I ordered for Jack."

Her hair fell over her shoulders, and Cole raked his fingers through it. "Online, what?"

Sara looked over her shoulder at him in confusion. "What?"

Cole gave her an evil smile. "The correct response is 'Online, Master.' Try again."

Sara took a deep breath. "Online. Master."

Cole grinned. "Better. Now, Jeremy, what are we going to do with this picture of submission?"

Jeremy was holding in his laughter. Sara knew she hadn't been very submissive so far. She really did want this, but it was hard to put away the Mistress mantle she had worn only minutes before.

"We're going to fuck this little slave, Cole. Hard and at the same time. But first I think we could use a little fluffing."

Sara looked down, and nothing could have been further from the truth. Both men were hard despite the fact they had already come once tonight. Her pussy tingled and her ass clenched at the thought of being fucked together. She had read so many books about it, but it looked like she was going to experience it for herself.

Jeremy gave a lordly wave toward the floor. "Kneel, slave, and suck our cocks."

Sara lowered her eyes submissively. "Yes, Masters."

Sara carefully knelt on the floor, and Jeremy's hand came out to steady her as she lowered herself with her hands still tied behind her back. The men came close to her, one on each side of her head. It appeared that she would be sucking them both and without the benefit of her hands.

She turned her head toward Jeremy. He pushed his cock toward her mouth, and she eagerly sucked him in, lapping at him with her tongue. She heard his groan of pleasure.

"Damn, her mouth is lethal. She sucks my cock as good as you do, baby."

She licked and sucked for a minute before turning toward Cole. His cock was ready and waiting for her mouth. She lapped at him like an ice cream cone until he tangled his fingers in her hair and gently tugged her where he wanted her mouth.

"Suck me, slave."

She went back and forth between the men for several minutes, their panting and groans amping up her own arousal. She was the only one that hadn't come yet tonight, and she was getting desperate.

They finally pulled away and walked a few steps back.

"You must be extremely aroused, slave. You have not had any release tonight. In fact, when was the last time you had release?"

Sara blushed. She wasn't sure she should tell them about her masturbation in the shower earlier today. She had been so horny watching them get ready for the party she couldn't help herself.

"Today, Masters, in the shower."

They both scowled. Shit, she was in trouble apparently.

"You came without our permission? That is not allowed, little slave. Ten for your disobedience."

Sara almost came on the spot. The thought of being spanked was thrilling. She had been spanked a few more times since that first time with Cole. She loved it, and they knew it.

"Hand or paddle?"

Sara looked demurely at the floor. "Whatever my Masters wish is my wish."

"Cole, help her up and bend her over the edge of the bed. I'll get the paddle."

Cole helped her up and into position. Bent over, legs spread, ass in the air, and pussy on display, she could only imagine the picture she made. She hoped it was an arousing one to her men.

Jeremy came up behind her, stroking her ass cheeks. "Five from me and five from Cole, since you disobeyed us. You'll count these out, little slave. Understand?"

"Yes, Masters." Her voice was muffled in the bedcovers.

The waiting was terrible, and then Jeremy gave her the first stroke. It landed with a thud, and the impact sent her up on her toes. Pain bloomed on her ass, to be quickly followed by pleasure. She realized Jeremy was waiting.

"One!"

The next stroke was just as hard and just as arousing. It seemed as if her bottom cheeks were connected directly to her clit. She was on the edge of orgasm quickly.

"Two!"

He drew out the next three, making sure she felt each stroke of the paddle individually. By the time Jeremy handed the paddle to Cole, she was begging to come.

"Please, Masters! Please, I need to come!"

Cole stroked her sore ass cheeks. "Soon, little one. I think you might come just from the paddling. Let's see, shall we?"

She thought Cole might go easy on her compared to Jeremy, but if anything the paddle struck as smartly or more as before. Tears leaked as her sore ass throbbed with heat, sending waves of mini-orgasms through her pussy. She was actually coming from being paddled.

"You're not counting, slave. Does that mean you want another stroke in its place?"

"Six!"

The next stroke sent her into another climax, rippling through her cunt, sending cream gushing from her pussy.

"Seven!"

The next stroke sent a wave of pleasure-pain so strong her body tightened and her orgasm rolled over her. It racked her body, shooting through her like the fireworks earlier in the evening. She screamed their names and barely registered the two strokes from the paddle that completed her punishment. She only knew they kept her coming and coming long after she thought she couldn't take that much pleasure. Somewhere, the pain and pleasure combined and she floated until she finally opened her eyes, spent and replete. Her men were holding her close and murmuring words of praise and endearment.

"You are so amazing, Sara. God, we love you so much."

Cole pushed her hair out of her eyes. "Yes, we love you so much, princess. You're so perfect for us."

Sara blinked. "You love me?"

Cole smiled tenderly. "Of course. What do you think all of this is about? You're beautiful, strong, intelligent, funny, a great mom, and you love to play games with us. We'd be real boneheads if we didn't fall in love with you."

Jeremy chuckled. "Ditto what he said. Hell, double ditto."

Sara tried to push up, but her hands were still restrained behind her. "But you love each other. You can't love me."

Cole frowned. "Why not? Do you think there's a limit to how much love a home can hold? I love you as much as I love Jeremy."

Sara was in a daze. They couldn't really be saying this. "I can't believe what you're saying is true. I love you both so much. I tried not to, you know. But you're such good men. You make me laugh and smile. You're wonderful to Jack. And the games…" She rolled her eyes. "What can I say? They're just awesome."

Sara looked back and forth between these amazing men. Cole was her creative genius, always taking ideas to the next level. He could talk to her for hours about her ideas, thoughts, and dreams. So many times over those dark months he had teased and talked her out of her funk, making her feel like the only woman in the world.

Jeremy was her Rock of Gibraltar. He had been the one she had turned to when it had all seemed like too much to handle. His calm and in-charge demeanor made her feel safe and cared for.

Cole framed her face with his hands. "We do love you. We admit that we've been attracted to you for a long time. But these weeks with you have deepened our feelings. We love you, and we want you to stay."

Sara was choked with emotion. She wasn't sure she could truly stay. But she had this time with them now. She would make the most of it.

"I want to be with you. With both of you."

Jeremy grinned. "Now that sounds like a plan. Let's get you untied and riding Cole's cock."

* * * *

Jeremy was speechless at Sara's declaration of love. She hadn't said she would stay, but it was a start. His heart felt so full when he looked at her and Cole. They were everything to him, along with Jack. He finally felt his family was complete. He and Cole hadn't known they were missing something until they had Sara and Jack in their lives. Everything felt right now.

Cole lay down on the bed and donned a condom. Jeremy smiled at the thought of a day when neither would need to suit up. Perhaps they could talk Sara into another baby. A little blond boy or a dark-haired girl would be the ultimate gift, and Jack would love a playmate.

He untied her hands and massaged her shoulders as she swung her leg over Cole. Her wanted her relaxed for what they were about to do. He wouldn't be able to get inside her if she was tense.

"Relax, princess. Let Cole slide into that pretty pussy. How does it feel, Cole?"

Cole's expression of pleasure matched Sara's as inch after inch of Cole's dick disappeared inside her. "Her pussy feels so hot and tight, J. God, I love fucking her. She's going to feel even tighter when you burrow into her virgin ass."

Sara gave him an indignant look. "Who said I had a virgin ass? Why do men always assume a woman's never had anal sex?"

Cole gave her a devilish grin. "Sorry, honey. I shouldn't assume. It's great that you're not a virgin. Jeremy can just go ahead and slam into your ass and give you a good, hard fucking there."

Sara's cheeks turned red. "Wait! I am...I mean...shit. I am a virgin there. I just thought it was wrong to assume it. You should ask."

Jeremy couldn't stop the laughter that had bubbled up. She was just so damn cute.

"Don't worry, honey. I'm going to pop that cherry nice and slow. You're going to love it."

He grabbed the lube and placed his hand on the middle of her back, pressing her down onto Cole's chest. Cole started distracting her with nibbles, kisses, and roaming hands while Jeremy dribbled the lube down her crack. Her tight rosette peeked out from between the still-red globes of her ass. She was going to be a pleasure to fuck.

* * * *

Sara held her breath as Jeremy's fingers circled her back hole, spreading the lube. She felt his finger press on the tight ring of muscles, trying to gain entry.

"Breathe, princess, and push out against my finger. That's a good girl."

She pushed, and his finger slid in to the hilt. She waited for the burn she had always heard about, but it didn't come. It did feel strange, and her ass felt full. She wiggled on his finger, trying to get him to move.

He pulled his finger out, and she felt so empty. More lube was added, and this time she felt more fingers pushing for entry. She knew what to do this time and pushed out as his fingers pressed in. This time she felt the burn, but she didn't feel a lot of pleasure. The books seemed to think she should be climbing toward orgasm by now.

"I'm going to start stretching you, honey. Tell me if it hurts. I'm going to be very gentle."

She felt his fingers moving in her ass, stretching her tight back hole. She felt a bite of pain and almost told him to stop, but that was when the pleasure started. She moaned as his fingers ran over sensitive nerves while Cole's fingers played with her tight nipples. The sensations washing over her were almost too much.

"She likes it, J. Her pussy is clamping down on my cock like a fucking vise. I can't hold out forever here. Is she almost ready?"

Cole's voice sounded tense. She realized that he could feel Jeremy's fingers against his cock. The sensation must have been driving him crazy.

"Almost. Do you like my fingers in your ass, princess?"

Sara pressed her face into Cole's chest and nodded. "Yes. Yes, I do. It feels so full and decadent. It feels so naughty and dirty. I love it when it's dirty."

Cole's laughter rumbled in his chest. "You are full, honey. Full of cock and fingers. As for naughty and dirty? We must be doing it right, then, if it feels that way."

Jeremy removed his fingers, and she cried out at the feeling of loss. She needed something in her ass, and she needed it now, dammit.

"Easy, baby. I'm going to fuck you now. It's time for all of us to be together."

There was the crinkle of a condom wrapper, and then she felt the blunt head of his cock pressing against her ass for entrance. She pushed back to let him in, frantic to get her ass filled again. He pulled back then pressed forward—back and forth—until she had everything he could give her. He rubbed her shoulders and back, trying to relax her.

"Breathe, honey. You need to breathe. When you're ready, Cole and I will start moving and give you the fucking of your life."

Sara took a deep breath and then another. "Fuck me."

Boy, did they ever. They fucked her slowly in the beginning, building up speed as their cocks filled her holes and rubbed her clit. Desire washed through her bones, sending her spiraling higher and higher with each thrust. There wasn't a moment she wasn't stuffed full of cock—Cole's or Jeremy's. Cole's rubbed her clit and Jeremy's rubbed sensitive tissue in her ass. Their bodies were covered with sweat, their breath coming in pants, as they all moved closer to the climax.

"Now, Cole." Jeremy's voice sounded strained. Cole reached between them and rubbed her clit. It was all she needed to send her over the edge. She screamed her completion as her men continued to pound into her. The force of her orgasm threw her down into Cole's chest as Jeremy thrust inside her and stilled. She was amazed at how clearly she could feel his cock jerk and spasm as he filled the condom with his cum.

Cole pressed inside her and froze. His face was contorted with painful passion, and his body tightened. He, too, filled the condom with his hot seed. They all collapsed in a heap of arms and legs, too tired and sated to move.

It was Jeremy who moved first, gently pulling from her sore ass. She had been soundly paddled and fucked and was sure to be sore tomorrow. Jeremy returned from taking care of the condom to lift her carefully off of Cole. He laid her down on the comforter and used a warm washcloth to clean her up. She tried to protest in embarrassment, but Jeremy persisted.

"We won't have any of that, princess. You're ours now."

She could barely keep her eyes open as Jeremy cuddled up to her back and Cole to her front. She had never been this happy and satisfied. If only it could last forever.

Chapter 12

"When are we going to tell her?"

Cole poured himself a cup of coffee and looked out onto the back patio, where Sara and Jack were playing with his new police car. Last night had been the most amazing and wonderful of Cole's life. They had told Sara how they felt, and she had returned their feelings. Things were coming together for them, and Cole didn't want anything to ruin it.

Jeremy slumped against the kitchen counter. "Today. After we take Jack to playgroup, we'll tell her." Jeremy followed Cole's gaze to the patio. "I've decided to pay for Stacey's college. She's Scott's daughter and my niece. It seems like the right thing to do."

Cole wrapped an arm around Jeremy's shoulders, pulling him close for a soft kiss. "You're amazing, you know that? I love you so fucking much. It's absolutely the right thing to do. She's family."

Jeremy shook his head. "Don't put me on a white horse, baby. It did cross my mind to shred that file and pretend we never talked to Alex. But shit, I just can't do that."

"I doubt you were tempted for long. You're too good a man to do that. Sara needs to know that Jack has a half sister. We're doing the right thing."

Jeremy's eyes looked sad. "This is going to hurt her, and there isn't a fucking thing we can do to stop it."

"We can be there for her, J. Sara's a strong woman. She's proved that in the last year and a half. She'll be okay. She has us and she has Jack."

Jeremy gave him a crooked smile. "I hope that's enough. I hope we're enough."

* * * *

Sara stretched out on the chaise lounge on the patio. Jack was at playgroup, and Cole and Jeremy had left for work a few hours ago. She was looking forward to some quality time with her e-reader and the latest erotic ménage story by her favorite author.

She smiled as thoughts of the night before drifted through her mind. The men said they loved her and wanted her to stay. She loved them, too. She hadn't expected to fall in love when she came here. It had been the furthest thing from her mind, actually. But here she was, in love with two wonderful men. They made her happy and they made Jack happy. How could she have resisted?

She sipped her iced tea and sighed. Any relationship was fraught with difficulties, but this one would be off the charts. First, one of the men was the brother of her late husband. That was different right there. Second, well, there were two of them. She wasn't sure this little town was ready for a ménage trio raising a toddler. Third, she lived in Florida. Her home, friends, and job were there. She wasn't sure about picking her life up and moving here for a relationship, even one as amazing as this one. She had lived in Florida her entire life. She didn't even own a winter coat or gloves.

The sound of the front door opening startled her, and she turned to see Jeremy and Cole heading out to the patio. Sara frowned. They shouldn't be home for several hours yet.

"Are you guys okay? Are you sick?"

They both smiled and gave her a kiss. Cole grabbed her hand and gave it a squeeze. "We're fine, princess. We missed you today."

"You came home early because you missed me?" Sara laughed. "I think I know why. Last night wasn't enough for you, huh?"

Jeremy smiled and held her other hand. "Last night was the greatest night of our lives. We hope that we have a lifetime of nights with you, Sara. But we came home to talk to you. There's something we have to tell you, and we wanted to be alone with you when we did."

Sara felt dread beginning to build in the pit of her stomach. They looked like they'd rather be anywhere but here talking to her.

"So talk to me. Jack's at playgroup." Her voice came out shaky.

Both men pulled chairs forward and sat down. Jeremy pulled a folder from his briefcase.

"This is about the bank account Scott had. It doesn't have anything to do with the business."

Sara frowned. "It doesn't? Then what is it for?"

Jeremy swallowed heavily before glancing at Cole. "Scott was sending two thousand dollars a month to a family here in Champaign for the last several years."

Her heart was pounding so loudly she was sure that Jeremy and Cole could hear it. She didn't want to ask, but she knew she had to. "Why? Why was he sending the money to someone? Oh shit, was he gambling again?"

Tears welled up in her eyes. She had thought Scott quit playing cards when they got married.

Cole shook his head and squeezed her hand. "No, he wasn't gambling, princess. He was sending the money to his daughter. Scott had a daughter he didn't know about until a few years ago. He was helping support her."

Sara felt Cole's words like a blow to her heart. She looked at Jeremy. "Is this true? Scott has a daughter?"

Jeremy scraped his hands across his face. "Yes. Scott had a daughter by his high school sweetheart. A daughter he never knew about until about five years ago. He didn't cheat on you, Sara."

Sara felt the anguish turn to anger. "Well, that's okay then. He didn't cheat on me. Hey, he only lied to me. That's not so bad. My beloved husband was a fucking liar!"

Sara jumped up from the lounge chair and began to pace. Jeremy stood, too, and tried to grab her hand, but she shook him off.

"I'm sure he had his reasons. We'll never know why or if he intended to tell you one day. He did have a sense of obligation to his daughter, and for that he should be respected."

Sara stopped and turned toward Jeremy slowly. She couldn't believe her ears. "What are you saying, Jeremy? That I should admire my late husband? That I should just forgive and forget that he was living a lie? What else don't I fucking know about Scott? What else?"

Sara screamed the last words, and the tears started to fall. The pain of Scott's passing felt so fresh suddenly. It was like he had died all over again. Cole pulled her into his arms, stroking her hair.

"Shhhh, princess. No, we don't think you should admire Scott for this. He should have told you. Jeremy wasn't defending him, just trying to explain the situation. If you want to get mad, you go right ahead. We'll be here while you scream and throw things. We'll always be here for you."

Sara wiped her hand across her tearstained cheeks. Salty tears had run into her mouth, and she needed a tissue. She turned to Jeremy. "Did you know? How long have you known?"

Jeremy's face turned white. "Fuck, no, I didn't know. Not until yesterday. When Steve didn't know anything about the account, I hired a friend. He's a private investigator. He found the information for us and brought it yesterday. We didn't want to ruin Jack's birthday by telling you. We decided to wait until today."

Sara smiled bitterly. "Well, thank you for that at least. So you've known there was something up for a while then, didn't you? This man didn't find all this out in one day."

Cole wiped her still-wet cheeks with his handkerchief. "We suspected something last week, but we didn't know anything for sure.

There was no point getting you all upset if it was nothing. I'm sorry it wasn't nothing, honey. I wish it was. We would do anything to keep you from hurting."

Sara tried to keep her emotions under control. Crying wasn't going to get her anywhere. "Does that folder contain the details?" She held her hand out.

Jeremy handed it to her. "Yes. Everything we know is in there. I wish Alex had found something else, but he didn't. I'm so sorry that we had to tell you. I'm just so fucking sorry."

Sara sat back down and opened the folder. "I'd like to be alone, please. I need to be alone right now."

Cole and Jeremy exchanged a worried look. It was clear they didn't want to leave her alone. She didn't give a fuck right now. She needed to read this file, and she knew that she couldn't do it when they were there. She needed privacy.

"I mean it, boys. I need to be alone right now. I'll be okay."

Their shoulders slumped in defeat and they headed into the house but not before giving her a soft kiss on each cheek.

"We love you, princess." Jeremy stroked her jaw.

Cole lifted her fingers to his lips. "Love you more than you can imagine. Just call us if you need us. We'll be in the house."

Sara nodded and turned away. The knot in her stomach wasn't going away anytime soon. She picked up the first page of the folder and began to read the report.

* * * *

Sara sat back in the chair and rubbed her aching temples. She had read and reread every word in the file, looked at every picture, and yet it still seemed surreal. Her husband had literally had a secret life. In some respects, he had a second family he spent two weeks out of every month with. The file had made clear that he hadn't been unfaithful, but it was cold comfort. Her husband had lied to her. Not a silly lie like he got drunk at a strip club or gambled away the grocery money on a horse. This was a great big lie.

A lie for no fucking reason. She wouldn't have been angry with Scott. It had all happened years before he met her. She would have been shocked, but she wouldn't have divorced him. She loved her husband. Of course, now she couldn't help but wonder what else he had lied about. What had he taken to his grave?

A huge part of their marriage was fiction. The trust she had based their lives on was crumbling sand. Sara was torn between grief and anger. She had loved Scott unconditionally. He had apparently not believed in that love. She wanted to scream at him, beat at his chest, and ask him why. Why? Why? She would never have that answer, and that was the most infuriating thing of all. He had left her, alone, and in the dark, about so many things.

She gathered the scattered papers and photos and placed them one by one back in the folder. She lingered on the photo of Scott's daughter. She looked very much like Scott and a little like Jack, too. Jack had a half sister, and she had precious few years with her father, too. No one came out of this unscathed. The report said that Stacey and Scott had grown very close. All the while, he had been coming home and acting as if nothing else was going on in his life. It was unreal.

She glanced at the report and zeroed in on one particular piece of information. She knew what she had to do. Sitting around feeling sorry for herself was not an option. She gathered up the file and headed through the living room, grabbing her purse. Jeremy and Cole were each nursing a beer in the kitchen.

"I'm going for a drive. I shouldn't be gone long, but if I'm not back, can you pick up Jack?"

They both jumped up from the kitchen table. "You shouldn't go alone, princess. I'll come with you." Cole grabbed for his car keys, but she put up her hand to halt him.

"No. I'm going alone. I need to do this myself."

Jeremy opened his mouth to object, but she shook her head.

"No, Jeremy. I. Need. To be. Alone. I love both of you, but I need to be by myself. Don't worry. I'm not going to do something drastic. I'm going for a drive."

Both men sat down in defeat. Cole gave her a hopeful look. "Be careful, and call us in a little while? Just to let us know you're okay."

Sara gave him a weak smile. "Yes. I'll call you when I'm in a little better head space. Just please don't forget Jack."

Jeremy nodded. "Don't worry about Jack. We'll take care of him. We'll take care of you, too, if you let us. We love you."

Sara headed for the door and couldn't look back. Her heart ached with love for them and grief for Scott.

"I love you, too. I'll be back soon."

Chapter 13

Sara sat in the car looking across the street at the home of Scott's other family. With the address in the file, and GPS in Jeremy's car, the red-brick bungalow on a quiet Urbana street had been easy to find. It was a hot summer day, and the mother and daughter were in the front yard weeding and watering the small flower garden. A cocker spaniel danced around at their feet, in and out of the water streaming from the hose. The dog shook, spraying water all over, and they laughed before tossing a ball into the backyard. The dog took off after it.

Sara lost track of time as she sat in the car watching them. She tried to picture Scott taking part in their family activities—planting flowers, sweeping the porch, maybe painting the mailbox. She shook her head. Scott had never done those activities with her, so it was difficult to imagine his interaction here. When he had been home, he worked, played softball, watched sports, or maybe read a book to relax.

Her hand went to the door handle. She had so many questions for this woman. Yes, she wanted to know why Scott had never told her. But mostly she wanted to know the Scott that had spent time here. She wanted to know if he had been the same or different as the Scott that came home to her and Jack. Had there been a part of him that Sara couldn't fulfill? A part of her wanted to believe that this Scott was somehow different or separate from her Scott, but most of her knew there was only one Scott. One Scott who had successfully lived two lives for years.

The mother brought out two cans of Coke and handed one to the girl. She said something, and they both laughed. Sara couldn't help the smile that spread across her face, too. She looked so much like Scott. Sara's heart ached and yet felt the same joy as she did when she looked at Jack. It was like having a part of Scott with her always.

Her hand fell away from the door. It wasn't right. The woman had said she never wanted anything from Sara. All she had wanted was to live in peace with her daughter. Sara knew she couldn't intrude. Someday, when Jack was older, he might want to seek out his sister. But today…today there was nothing to be gained by Sara exiting the car and introducing herself. She might get a few answers, but inevitably it would only create more questions. There wasn't an answer that would make her feel any better anyway.

She leaned back on the headrest and felt the hot tears leak from her eyes. She cried for Scott, whose life was cut so very short. She cried for Jeremy, who had lost his brother. She cried for that beautiful girl who had found her father and lost him so quickly. She cried for herself and the loss of the life she and Scott had dreamed about. And finally, she cried for Jack, who would never know his father.

When she finally ran out of tears, she reached for the ignition and started the car. She may not have gotten all the answers she came for, but she got enough. It wasn't all about her. It was about Scott's two children.

She pulled away from the curb and headed back to Jeremy and Cole. The next few hours weren't going to be easy, but she knew what she needed to do.

* * * *

Sara pushed the front door open and almost ran into Jeremy and Cole. Jeremy had Jack in his arms. They must have been watching out the front window for any sign of her return. Sara pulled Jack from Jeremy's arms and kissed and cuddled him until he giggled. She looked at his sweet face, and her heart swelled with love. Her most important job was Jack's mother.

"Princess, are you okay? We tried calling you." Cole wrapped his arms around her and pulled her close. Jeremy lifted Jack from her arms and set him down on the living room floor with his toys.

Sara pushed on his chest. She needed some space at the moment. "I'm fine. I'm really okay. I didn't hear the phone."

Jeremy pushed a wayward strand of hair back from her face. "Where were you, honey?"

"I went to see Scott's other family."

She knew the statement would shock them. Jeremy's face paled, and Cole pulled her down on the couch and sat next to her.

"I wish you would have talked to us about that first. We would have gone with you, Sara." Jeremy's voice was gentle, but she could see the fear in his eyes. He was wondering if she had done something really stupid.

Cole shook his head, his expression a little angry. "He didn't have another family. You and Jack were his family."

Sara struggled for words. She wanted to say this right. "Yes, he did. He spent half of the last four years here with them. I get that now, and I get why."

Cole started to protest, but she held up her hand. "It's okay, Cole. It was his daughter. She deserved to have a father just as much as Jack did. And I didn't talk to them, by the way. I just drove to the house and watched them for a little while. I realized they wouldn't have the answers to my questions. Only Scott has those."

The last was directed at Jeremy, whose jaw was set in a grim line. He wiped a hand down his face in relief.

"You did the right thing, honey. If you want to talk to them, I can have Alex set something up with them."

Sara shook her head. "Someday when Jack is older I'll tell him he has a sister and let him decide. In the meantime, Alex can let them know that I'm open to it if they want to meet Jack. This isn't about what I want anymore. This is about what is best for the children."

Jeremy sat on her other side and held her hand. "What can we do to make this better, honey? How can we help?"

Their faces were etched with worry. It made what she had to say all the harder. She truly loved these men. She hadn't planned it, but there it was. Jeremy was strong and steady. She could rely on him in any situation, even one as bad as this one. Cole was her mad genius. He could see life in ways she barely imagined. Everything he did, he took to the next level, including his love for her. Both men loved Jack, too. She really hadn't stood a chance at not falling in love with them.

"You can't help me. I have to deal with this on my own." She placed a hand on each of theirs. "That's why Jack and I are leaving tomorrow. We're going home."

* * * *

Jeremy's chest tightened in panic at Sara's words, but he tried to keep his voice calm and even. "I don't understand, honey. Why are you leaving?"

Sara stood up and began to pace. She finally sat next to Jack on the floor, running her fingers through his unruly locks.

"I need some time to deal with this. I need to process everything that has happened these last weeks—being with you and finding out about Scott. It's a lot, and I need some time to decide how to move forward from here."

Jeremy crouched next to her, and Jack began to climb up Jeremy's torso. He hugged Jack's little body close. He smelled of peanut butter and baby powder. Jeremy and Cole had gotten used to the crumbs and the chaos of having a toddler in the house. Jeremy knew he didn't want to go back to the way it was before.

"Can't you do that here? Why do you have to leave me and Cole to deal with this?"

Sara looked him straight in the eye. "Because I can't. Right now I don't know whether I love or hate Scott. I'm mad at him and mad at myself for not knowing what was going on. I thought I had dealt with his death and moved on with my life. But this brought all my emotions back to the surface, dammit. I have to deal with those emotions before I can deal with my emotions for both of you."

Sara's voice had softened, and she reached for Cole's hand, too. "It doesn't mean I don't love you. I do love you. Both of you. But let's face it, Jeremy, what future did we have anyway? You two are already in a relationship. With each other. You don't need me."

Jeremy's heart felt like it was being ripped from his chest. Apparently, they hadn't made their feelings clear enough.

"Cole and I fucking need you, Sara. You and Jack. We want to be a family with you, dammit. A forever family."

Cole looked ravaged. "Princess, we love you. Please don't leave us. You're a part of us now. Both you and Jack are our hearts." His voice sounded thick with emotion. Jeremy threw his other arm around his husband. He could feel how tensely Cole was holding himself.

Sara was not unmoved. Her eyes were bright with unshed tears. "God, I love both of you. Jack adores you. But, please, I need some time. Just a little time." Sara choked on the last word. How could they refuse her?

Jeremy pulled her close, holding her and Jack in his arms. Jack wriggled and protested until Jeremy let him go. Jack ran to his toys and picked up a train.

"Choo choo! Play choo choo!"

Jeremy held back the emotion that flooded him at the thought of Sara and Jack leaving. But she was asking for time. She hadn't asked them for much, and they really didn't have a choice.

"If you want to go home, Sara, we won't stop you." Cole started to protest, but Jeremy squeezed his shoulder.

Sara wiped a single silvery tear from her cheek. "I don't want to go, but I feel like I have to. I need space to think things through."

Jeremy nodded. "We'll take you to the airport tomorrow if that's what you want. But please don't think there's no future for you here. This is your future, and you are our future. We want to be with you. Cole and I have been happy, but the three of us are something greater, something more. You make us whole."

Cole leaned forward and gave Sara a hard kiss. "Fucking forever. That's how long we want you. We'll let you go. For now. But this isn't the end, princess. Not by a long shot."

Sara picked up the train and began playing with Jack. After a few minutes, she turned and gave them a small smile. "Thank you. I just need some time."

Jeremy gripped Cole's hand and bit his lip to keep from begging her to stay. She was a strong woman, and they needed to believe in her. Now more than ever.

Chapter 14

Sara sat in the semidarkness of her lanai. The only sounds were crickets and the creaking of the ceiling fan overhead. It had been a pretty miserable month, and she was utterly exhausted by the gamut of emotions she had experienced.

Jeremy and Cole had driven her and Jack to the Indianapolis airport that next morning. It had been a grim journey broken only by Jack's chattering and Cole and Jeremy trying to entertain him. When it had been time for her and Jack to go through security and Jeremy and Cole couldn't follow, Jack had thrown a major tantrum. The toddler didn't understand why Jeremy and Cole weren't coming, too. It was all Sara could do to hold him in her arms. She practically dragged him through passenger screening and then into the waiting area. She had finally calmed him down before getting on the plane. She knew Jack loved her men so much. Her own heart was breaking. She wanted to throw herself down and cry, too.

Tori, Lisa, Brianne, and Noelle had practically met her at the front door of her home when the airport taxi dropped her and Jack off at the house. Brianne was carrying her infant daughter, Paige Marie Hart. Paige had Nate's dark hair and piercing blue eyes and Brianne's delicate features. She was sure to be a beauty when she got older. Brianne nursed Paige while Sara told them the whole story, leaving no detail out. These were her best friends after all. By the time she was done, she was emotionally drained, but her burden felt lighter. Her friends were there for her once again as they had been when Scott died.

They had hugged her, encouraged her, and, the next day, stood by her when she called on the therapist that she had seen a few times after the funeral. Talking to someone who was neutral in the situation had helped immensely.

Jeremy and Cole still Skyped each Sunday. Each call was stilted and awkward, with so much unsaid between them. A part of her wanted to run back to them and let them make everything all better, another part knew she needed to be whole before she went back to them. Assuming, of course, they even wanted her back. They had been perfectly fine before her, and they would be perfectly fine with her gone. They were probably already enjoying the peace and quiet of their home without her and Jack around. No toys to trip over, no crumbs to clean up, no tantrums to soothe.

Her phone jangled next to her, and she reached to pick it up. Noelle.

"Hey, Elle. Are you okay? You're calling late."

"I was up working on a design." Noelle was a talented jewelry designer. "I was also watching that chick movie. You know, the one where the two people hate each other and then fall in love."

Sara chuckled at Noelle's description. It could fit any number of chick movies.

"And that made you think of me? How…nice."

"Stay with me here." Sara could almost see Noelle's eye roll. "It made me think about people at cross-purposes. So, here's the thing. Fucking call them, Sara."

"I can't."

"Wow, you said that quick. Call. Them. What are you waiting for? You love them, they love you. Yeah, this Scott thing was a kick on the ass, so to speak, but life goes on. You going to sit around feeling sorry for yourself because your husband turned out to not be perfect?"

This was so like Noelle. She was a grab-life-by-the-balls kind of person.

"I'm not feeling sorry for myself. I'm just processing things."

"Still? How long are going to *process* things? Just so you know, life is happening in the background while you do that. You'll never get these days back. They're gone. Poof! So you don't know why Scott kept the secret? Tough shit. Is there any reason he could have that would make this okay for you?"

No. There wasn't any reason that would make this okay. She was coming to the conclusion that it would be best to never know what feeble excuse Scott had.

"I may not have ever been married, Sara, but I do know one thing. We don't really fucking know people. Yeah, we think we do. We get married, and have babies, and live with them, and we think that gives us some special insight into their soul. Bull hockey. It doesn't. People always have a little something they keep to themselves. Did Scott know every single, freakin' thing about you? Shit, he didn't even know the kind of reading material you liked."

Sara opened her mouth to say he did, but closed it instead. It wouldn't be true. As much as they had loved each other, and had a wonderful marriage, they didn't know every single thing about each other, and wouldn't have even if they'd been married for fifty years.

"You're such a sensitive friend, Elle. You should be a therapist."

Noelle burst out laughing. "You have a therapist. Now you need some tough love. Let's face it. I'm the perfect friend for it. I was duly deputized by the group."

Ah, her friends had elected Noelle to do the dirty work. Typical.

"I'll think about it, okay? I don't like being like this either, you know."

"Good. Now I need to get back to work. Stop calling me so late at night, woman. Get some sleep."

Sara hung up the phone laughing at Noelle's parting joke. She had definitely planted a seed. A seed of hope.

* * * *

Cole lay awake staring at the red glow of the alarm clock on the bedside table. The numbers read two in the morning. He hadn't been sleeping well since Sara left. Jeremy, either. It was hard to sleep with a broken heart. They knew Sara needed this time, but they didn't have to like it. It was hard as hell not to hop the next airplane and bring her home.

They both missed her warm little body between them. They missed her smile, her laugh, her sharp intelligence, and her penchant for playing games. Mostly, they missed the way she completed them. She was the bridge between them. He and Jeremy were so different yet so the same. She complemented them perfectly.

They missed Jack, too. The house seemed so quiet with their little boy gone. Every day they said they were going to pack up the police car they had bought Jack for his birthday and send it to Florida, and every day they didn't do it. They still had hope he and Sara would come back.

He felt Jeremy's hand stroke his shoulder. "You okay, baby?"

Cole turned in to Jeremy's arms. "Yeah. Just miss her. You, too?"

"You know I do." Jeremy's voice was rough with sleep. "Jack, too. She said she needed time."

Cole pressed his lips to Jeremy's. "I know. Have we given her enough time now?"

Jeremy pulled him tighter. "I don't know. I do know I'm tired of waiting. What if we go after her and she doesn't love us anymore? What if every time she sees me, she sees Scott? I couldn't live with myself if I brought her more pain."

Cole sat up in the bed. "There's only one way to know, J. Let's go get her and Jack. In the morning."

"Are you fucking serious? Just fly down there and tell her we're tired of waiting?"

"Yep. Listen, the worst is not knowing. If she doesn't want us anymore, we just fucking need to find out and move on. Although, I don't know how the hell we're going to do that."

Cole waited as the silence stretched on. Jeremy was the cautious one of them.

"We leave in the morning. Let's go tell her how much we love her and Jack."

Cole lay back down and cuddled with Jeremy. Now he was too excited to sleep. They were heading to see and hold their woman.

* * * *

Sara breathed in the scent of hibiscus and lilac. The air was heavy with humidity this time of year, but she still loved sitting on the lanai when she needed to think. It had become a place of refuge these last weeks. Today was no exception. Noelle's call the night before had given her a lot to think about.

For the first time in months, Jeremy and Cole didn't call on Sunday morning. At first she had thought they were just late, but hours had now passed. They weren't calling. They didn't want her after all. She had waited too long. Noelle had come by and offered to take Jack to the park. How Noelle had known that Sara needed time to herself she would never know, but she had gratefully agreed. A wash of love surged through her as she thought of her son. He looked like Scott. And Jeremy, too. They had all been so happy this summer. It had felt like a family again. She craved that peace and closeness. She craved the feeling of belonging. She needed it. Not just for her but for Jack, too. She owed him that.

She didn't like the woman she was becoming these last weeks. She was acting like a victim, and she hated that shit. She hated letting Scott affect her like this. She had loved him, but he was gone now. Why he had kept secrets from her, she didn't know. She would never know. She had blessed and released those unanswered questions. Getting the answers wouldn't make a damn bit of difference. So why was she sitting here feeling sorry for herself? She knew what she wanted. She couldn't be too much of a coward to go after her future. Noelle was right. She needed to stop sitting around and do something.

Sara jumped to her feet and headed into the house. She wouldn't give up on them. She wasn't going to sit back and let life happen to her. She was going to go out and grab it. Her friends would expect nothing less. She would propose a whole new game to her men. One that involved a lifetime together.

She reached for her phone. She was halfway through dialing when she heard pounding on the door. Noelle hadn't been gone very long. Apparently, Noelle had also forgotten the spare key she always carried.

Sara threw open the door impatiently.

"Elle, where's your k—" Sara stopped in shock. It was Jeremy and Cole on the other side of the door. They looked handsome, sexy, tired, and very, very determined. *Thank God.*

"Who's Elle?" Cole pushed past her carrying a gigantic suitcase, followed by Jeremy, who also carried a suitcase.

"Uh, my friend. She took Jack to the park."

Both men headed for the bedroom, with Sara trailing behind.

"What are you doing here? Where are you heading with those suitcases? Shit, answer me!"

Jeremy whirled around, his eyes narrowed with challenge. "We're here for you. We got tired of waiting. Whatever you need to deal with, we'll deal with it together. No more going it alone. As for where we're heading? The bedroom, honey. Cole and I are moving in."

Sara felt hope take root in her heart for the first time in weeks.

"For me? Moving in? What do you mean you're moving in?"

Shut up, Sara. This is what you want.

Cole threw the suitcases on the floor. "We're moving in, princess. If you won't come to us, we'll come to you. We're not going to be separated from you again. Period."

"Period? What about the business? Your home?"

Jeremy shook his head and pulled her close. She could smell his woodsy scent and feel the warmth of his skin. She had never thought she would feel these arms around her again. Her body was responding as it always did—preparing itself for their loving.

Cole came up behind her and kissed the back of her neck. "We'll explain it all, babe. But what we need to know is how much time we have before your friend brings Jack home."

Sara knew the look on her men's faces. She wanted the same damn thing.

"We've got about an hour, give or take. So we better get moving."

Chapter 15

Her men didn't need to be told twice. She was stripped of her shorts and tank top before she could catch her breath. Her bra and panties followed quickly after. She tried to work at their clothes, too, but they were determined to kiss and touch her everywhere. Her mind became a haze of pleasure, each stroke of their fingers or swirl of their tongues sending desire dancing through her veins.

They pushed her back onto the bed, lowering her gently to her back on the crisp sheets. Cole kissed her deeply, letting his tongue run wild inside her mouth. His fingers plucked at her nipples, twisting slightly, giving her the bite she loved so much. He ran his tongue down her neck and around her nipples. Sara arched her back, offering her breasts to his wicked mouth. He accepted the invitation. His tongue swirled around the tips before sucking a nipple in his mouth and gently scraping his teeth as he released it.

Jeremy kissed a wet trail of open-mouth kisses down her abdomen and between her thighs. He pushed her legs farther apart to make room for his wide shoulders. His tongue played along the strong muscles of her thighs before heading to her wet slit. She almost came off the bed when his tongue laved her sensitive clit.

"Your pussy is so pretty and pink, honey, and so wet and swollen for us. Do you want us to fuck you? I want to hear you say it."

She could feel his warm breath against her pussy. Her thighs were sticky with honey and her nipples were painfully tight. She needed these men badly.

Cole lifted his head from where he was licking and teasing a nipple.

"Best answer him, princess. You're not going to come until you do."

"That's mean." Sara's voice sounded breathless and aroused.

Cole's jaw tightened. "I ought to turn you over my knee for leaving us the way you did, so don't say this is mean. We just want to hear you say you want us. Say it, Sara."

Of course, she wanted them. Like her next breath.

"I want you. I want both of you. Please fuck me!"

Jeremy grinned up at her. "First, you need to come so I can lick up all this sweet cream."

He bent his head back to his task, tormenting her with his tongue. He ran along every crevice of her cunt, sending shivers of delight through her body and making her pussy clench with need, wanting something to fill it. Cole's mouth was on her breasts, sucking at the hard nubs, nipping with his teeth until she shuddered and moaned.

"Is she ready, Cole?"

"She's ready, baby. Make her come."

Jeremy's talented mouth latched onto her clit and sucked before raking his teeth gently across the swollen pearl. Her body bowed and then shattered into a thousand pieces of pleasure. Wave after wave racked her body, leaving her shaken and spent. Jeremy's mouth rode the waves with her, his tongue bestowing soft licks near the end as she came down from heaven.

When she opened her eyes, they were both staring down at her with expressions full of love. She was a lucky woman. She grinned. "I know what game I want to play next."

* * * *

Cole grinned back at his woman. Everything might not be perfectly worked out. Yet. But whatever she needed to deal with, they would deal with together. He and Jeremy were determined to help Sara through all the craziness the last few months had thrown at her.

Not the least of which was themselves. It had occurred to them at thirty thousand feet that being in love with, living with, and dealing with two men day in and day out might seem like a daunting task. After all, most women only had to put up with one man. Sara would have her hands full with the two of them. They promised then and there to make it as easy for her as possible.

"You know we love games, princess. Tell us what you have in mind." Cole glanced at Jeremy and saw the same mischief in his eyes. They loved her most of all for her mind—her absolutely brilliant and dirty mind.

Sara had an evil glint in her eye. "In the essence of getting done before Jack gets home, I think we should play the 'Jeremy and Cole fuck Sara at the same time' game."

Sara trailed her fingers across Jeremy's jaw. Cole was once again entranced by how much he loved these two people.

"I want us all to be together. So let's get down to business. We don't have much time. Grab the lube in the nightstand."

Sara pointed to the side of the bed with a determined look. Far be it for him to not give her the game she wished.

Cole and Jeremy pulled off the rest of their clothes. Jeremy pulled Cole close for a kiss. Their tongues and breath mingling, their hard cocks rubbing against each other made his dick painfully hard.

"That's so hot. I miss watching you two make love to each other. It's like my very own porn channel."

Jeremy quirked an eyebrow. "We're your personal porn, huh? Well, get the camera, because things are going to start heating up in this bedroom between the three of us."

Jeremy stretched out on the bed and beckoned to Sara. Cole helped her straddle Jeremy's legs. Cole breathed in her soft, floral scent and stroked her warm skin. He had missed her so much.

Cole snagged a couple of condoms from his pants pocket and tossed one to Jeremy. "Suit up, baby. I know we want her pregnant, but she has to agree to it first."

Sara looked from him to Jeremy in amazement. "You want a baby, too? I'd love to have another baby."

Cole's heart overflowed with love. "I love you so much, princess."

Sara gave them a sultry smile as she plucked the condom packet from Jeremy's fingers and tossed it on the nightstand. Unused and unneeded.

"I love you both. Let's get this game started."

* * * *

Sara couldn't believe what she was hearing. They still loved her, and they wanted to have a baby, too. She could picture a blonde little girl being held in their arms, or maybe another boy. It really didn't matter which actually. Maybe she could give them one of each.

She lowered herself slowly onto Jeremy's rock-hard cock. She was so wet, he slid in easily, rubbing delicious spots inside her with every ridge. She loved the way his cock felt without the barrier of the condom between them. When he was in to the hilt, she closed her eyes and tightened around him, feeling his dick pulse in her cunt. It sent sparks to her clit and more honey dripping from her pussy. She did it again, and he gripped her hips with a groan.

"Fuck, Sara. You're making me crazy."

She moved her hips from side to side and then up and down, experimenting to find just the right pleasure spot. She moaned as he rubbed a particularly sensitive area deep inside her. She felt Cole's chuckle behind her and his breath in her ear.

"Does his cock feel good, princess? He's so big, it's like he's reaching up and tickling your ribs, isn't it? I love it when he fucks me."

Sara nodded and moaned again as her movements rubbed his groin against her already-swollen clit. She needed to come again.

"She likes your big cock buried in her wet pussy, J. She's going to love my cock buried in her tight ass."

Sara's arousal built even higher at Cole's dirty talk. She wanted to enflame their desire as much as they did hers.

"Yes! Fuck my ass. Fuck my pussy, Jeremy. Give it to me hard. I need your big cocks," Sara panted.

Jeremy's eyes darkened with passion. "You're going to get all the cock you need, whenever you need it, honey. We're going to ride that sweet cunt and ass hard on a regular basis from now on so you don't forget where you belong or who you belong to. This pussy belongs to me and Cole now."

Cole tugged her head back and kissed her hard and long. "In case you're wondering where you belong, it's between us. Forever."

Cole pressed on the middle of her back until she was lying on top of Jeremy's chest. She felt Cole hands stroke her ass and then the cold trickle of lube run down her crack. She couldn't stop the shiver that went down her spine. She felt Cole freeze.

"Are you okay? Have you changed your mind?"

"No, of course not. It was just a little cold."

She heard Cole's slow exhale as he rubbed her back. "It'll warm up in a minute. Just relax for me, princess."

His fingers circled her tight hole, spreading the lube, before pressing for entry. She felt a moment of pressure and then his finger was inside her. More lube, and another finger was added. A third finger joined and then the scissoring. She could feel her ass stretch and loosen as he readied her for the fucking she was eagerly anticipating. She was already near orgasm at the thought of having both of her beloved men inside her at the same time.

Cole removed his fingers, and she mewled in frustration at the empty feeling he left behind.

"Easy, baby. I'm going to fuck you now. J, why don't you distract our princess a little?"

Jeremy stroked his hands down her back and up her rib cage to her breasts, kneading and caressing. She almost missed the sensation of Cole lining his cock up to her tight ass and pressing forward. Cole fed each hard inch of his cock into her ass relentlessly—pushing in, pulling out, then pushing in a little further each time. Each stroke ignited a fire that licked along her skin. She ground her clit against Jeremy, trying to find the right rhythm that would send her over the edge.

"Please, Cole, please fuck me. I need you both to fuck me now. I'm so close."

Cole hooked an arm around her waist and pulled her up against his chest.

"Yes, we're going to fuck you now."

Cole pulled back just a little and pushed forward one last time. This time he went in until his balls slapped her ass. She was completely full of cock. The feeling was unbelievable. She began to move. She needed more.

So frantic with desire, this fucking wasn't hesitant or gentle. This was passion, hot and hard, and so amazing. Her men were giving her all of themselves, and she returned the favor, becoming an instrument being played between them.

When Jeremy thrust into her, Cole pulled almost all the way out. When Cole slammed back into her ass, Jeremy pulled almost all the way out of her clenching pussy. She heard herself moaning and urging them on, telling them of her need and her love. They answered her back with a tempo that sent her over the edge. When she finally fell, she screamed her release. Her body shook with a pleasure almost painful in intensity.

Jeremy thrust into her one last time. She felt the jerking of his cock against her womb as he bathed her cunt with his cum. Cole followed the two of them over the cliff. His cock spasmed inside her tight ass, shooting his hot seed. They finally collapsed, sweaty and spent on the sheets.

It was Cole, as usual, who found his voice first. "I have to say, princess, that I do like your games. We'll have to put you on the payroll."

Sara felt Jeremy's laugh beneath her head. "These kinds of games would certainly make a fortune. I'm a fan."

The men pulled carefully from her and headed to the bathroom. Cole came out with a cloth to clean her up. She relaxed under his tender loving care.

Cole came back and stretched out next to her. "I don't mean to be the bearer of bad news, princess, but I think we have company."

Cole pointed out the window to the car parked next to their rental in the driveway. Noelle.

Oh shit, shit, shit.

Sara grabbed a robe and headed for the living room. How much had Noelle and Jack heard?

She almost collapsed in relief when she saw them playing in the backyard. Hopefully, they had been out there the whole time. Noelle looked up with an evil grin as Sara approached.

"My, my, Sara, looks like you have company. A couple of hunks if my eyes haven't deceived me."

Sara turned to see Jeremy and Cole heading straight for Jack, who was laughing and clapping his hands in delight. Luckily, they had both stopped to pull their clothes on. Still, Noelle wasn't stupid.

Sara looked at Noelle in question. Noelle shook her head. "I brought him straight back here. I saw the closed bedroom door and heard some heavy breathing and headed to the lanai. I thought you might appreciate the privacy."

Sara closed her eyes in relief. "I do, and thank you."

Jeremy and Cole were fussing over who was going to carry Jack. Sara turned back to Noelle. "I guess I should introduce you."

Noelle waved her off and headed for the front door. "Next time. It looks like you need some family time right now."

Sara nodded gratefully. Noelle was a wonderful friend. All her friends would have to meet her men.

"Stop spoiling him. I really mean it this time."

Sara put her hands on her hips and gave them a mock glare.

They just laughed at her. "Sorry, babe. I think he's going to be spoiled now that we've moved in here."

Sara liked the sound of that. "Just how is this going to work? You promised to explain it."

Cole pulled Jack from Jeremy's arms. Jeremy gave her a big smile. "We can work remotely, honey. I'll spend two weeks here a month and Cole will spend two weeks here a month. We'll overlap one of those weeks so you'll have someone with you three weeks out of the month. If we can swing it, maybe more."

Sara looked at them in amazement. "Don't you need to be in the office?"

"Congratulate Cole. He's been promoted. When I'm not in the office, he's in charge."

Cole smirked. "That's always been the case. He's just always in the office."

"I don't know what to say. I can't believe you're willing to move here."

"Jeremy and I want to be with you. This is hardly a sacrifice. We know you love your teaching job, and the school year starts very soon. Perhaps after the school year, we can decide if we still want to live here, in Illinois, or part-time in each place. We don't have to decide now. We have options. The important thing is we're together."

Sara's heart filled with love. Yes, the most important thing was the family they would build.

"So just how many babies do you boys want? I think I have a right to know."

Jeremy and Cole looked at her, their eyes twinkling. "Cole and I talked about it, and we want at least two more. Are you game to take us on? Make a family with us?"

Sara pulled her men close, one in each arm and Jack in the center of their circle.

"I'm game for a lifetime."

She prayed that was just what she would have with these amazing men, Jack, and their future children. Maybe, just maybe, Scott was up in heaven smiling down on them. She would always feel his love, remember their life together.

Today was a whole new beginning. Sara gave her boys a mischievous smile. "I have this idea for a new game. You see, I ordered some stuff online I think you'll really like."

THE END

WWW.LARAVALENTINE.NET

ABOUT THE AUTHOR

I've been a dreamer my entire life. So, it was only natural to start writing down some of those stories that I have been dreaming about.

Being the hopeless romantic that I am, I fall in love with all of my characters. They are perfectly imperfect with the hopes, dreams, desires, and flaws that we all have. I want them to overcome obstacles and fear to get to their happily ever after. We all should. Everyone deserves their very own sexy, happily ever after.

I grew up in the cold but beautiful plains of Illinois. I now live in Central Florida with my handsome husband, who's a real, native Floridian, and my son whom I have dubbed "Louis the Sun King." They claim to be supportive of all the time I spend on my laptop, but they may simply be resigned to my need to write.

When I am not working at my conservative day job or writing furiously, I enjoy relaxing with my family or curling up with a good book.

For all titles by Lara Valentine, please visit
www.bookstrand.com/lara-valentine

Siren Publishing, Inc.
www.SirenPublishing.com

CPSIA information can be obtained at www.ICGtesting.com
Printed in the USA
LVOW04s1701140615

442438LV00022B/820/P